essential careers™

CAREERS IN DENTISTRY

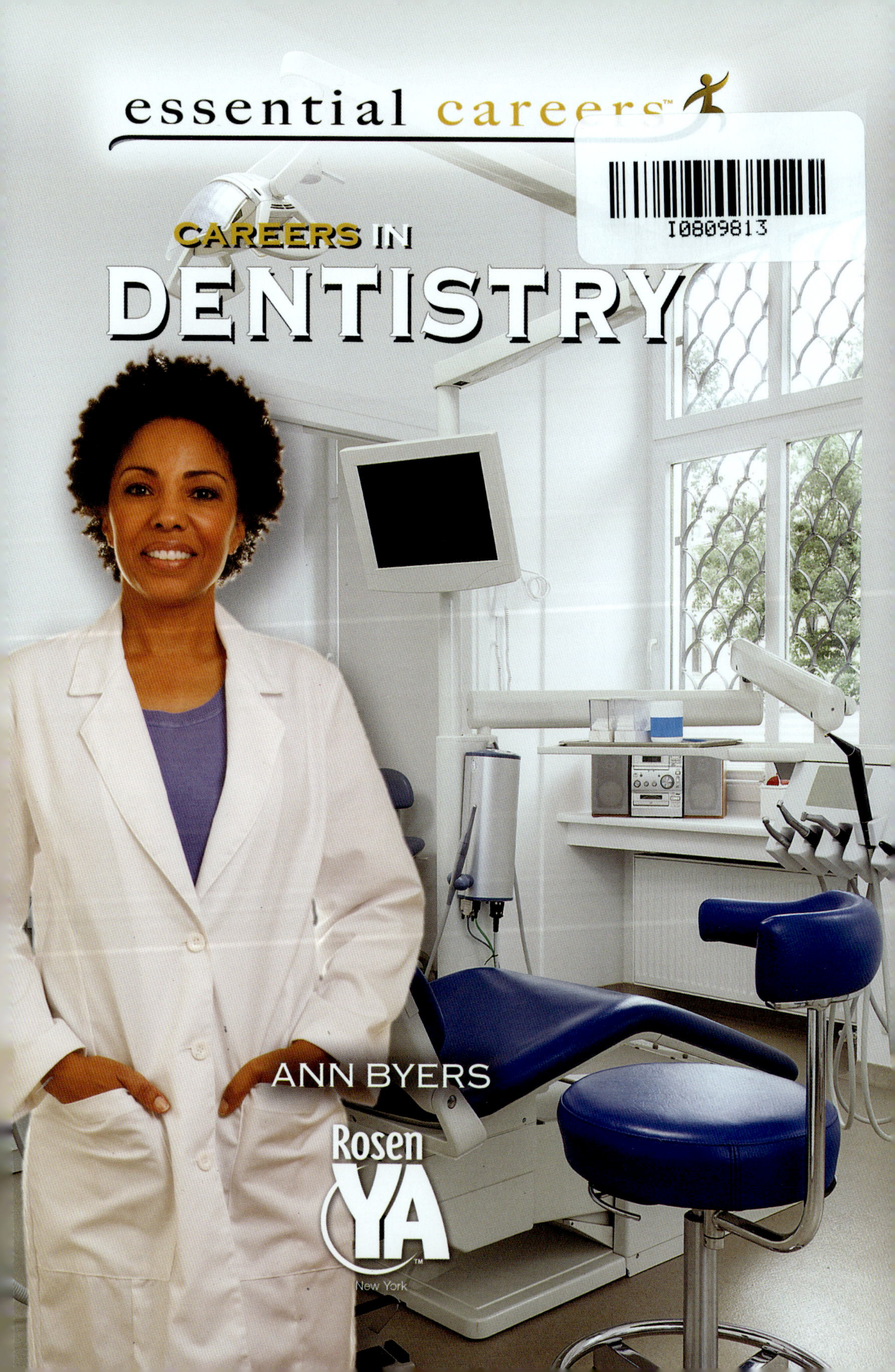

ANN BYERS

Rosen YA™
New York

Published in 2018 by The Rosen Publishing Group, Inc.
29 East 21st Street, New York, NY 10010

First Edition

Library of Congress Cataloging-in-Publication Data

Names: Byers, Ann, author.
Title: Careers in dentistry/Ann Byers.
Description: New York: Rosen Publishing Group, Inc., 2018. | Series: Essential careers | Audience: Grades 7–12. | Includes bibliographical references and index.
Identifiers: LCCN 2017014224 | ISBN 9781538381502 (library bound) | ISBN 9781508178842 (paperback)
Subjects: LCSH: Dentistry—Vocational guidance—Juvenile literature. | Dentists—Juvenile literature. | Dental assistants—Juvenile literature. | Dental hygienists—Juvenile literature.
Classification: LCC RK63 .B94 2018 | DDC 617.60023—dc23
LC record available at https://lccn.loc.gov/2017014224

Manufactured in China

contents

INTRO

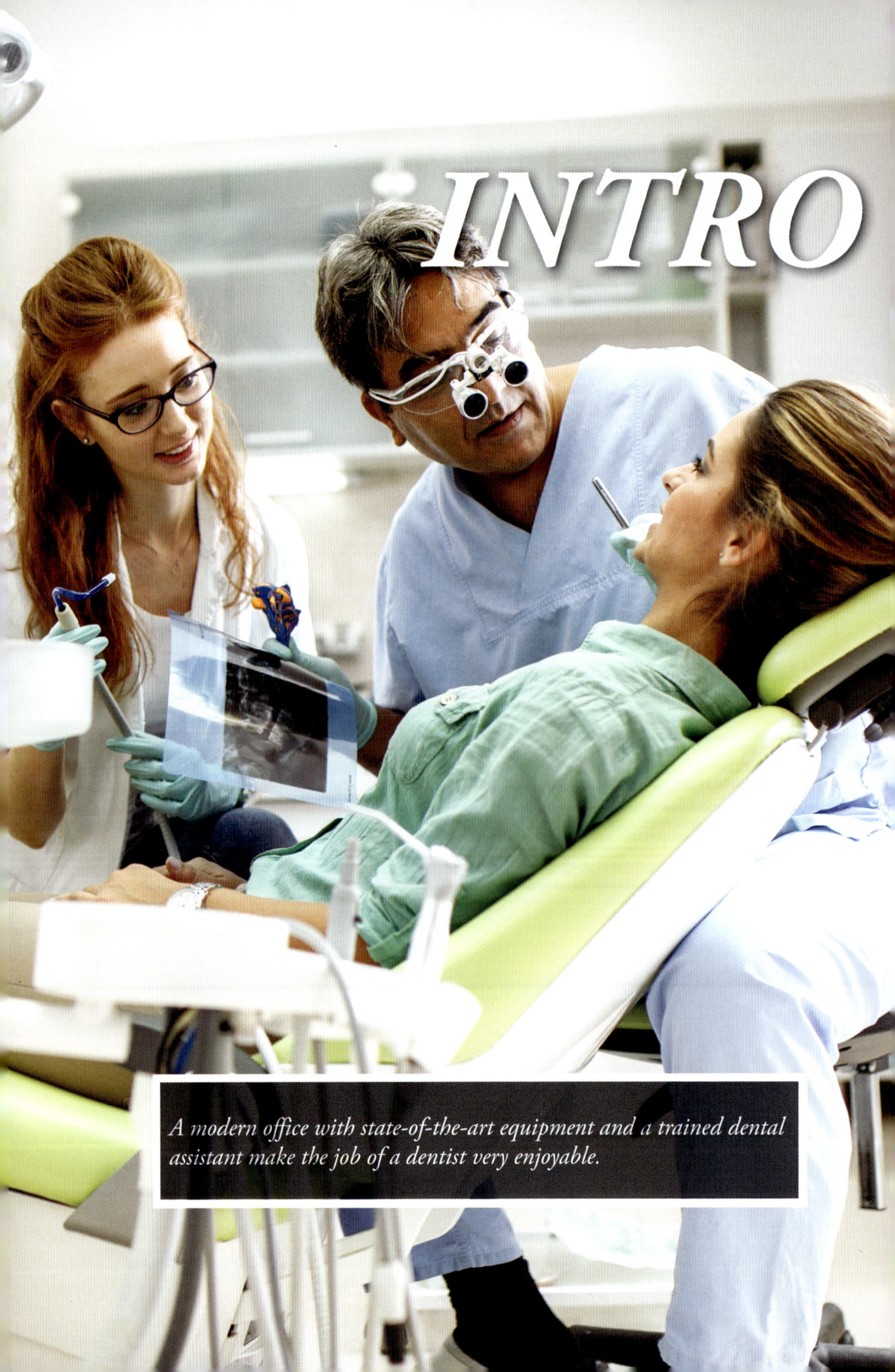

A modern office with state-of-the-art equipment and a trained dental assistant make the job of a dentist very enjoyable.

DUCTION

Mick Reynolds had a great job with a comfortable salary, but he wasn't happy. His work was important; as a manufacturing and plastics engineer, he designed airplane parts for a large corporation. Mick was detail-oriented, a problem solver, and he loved to create beautiful and useful things. But he went home from work bored and unsatisfied. Something was missing.

One day he discovered what that missing element was. His younger brother had recently become a dentist, and Mick watched him at work. His brother was something of an engineer like Mick; he worked with his hands to design physical solutions to problems. But he also interacted with people. Seeing his brother chatting cheerfully with his patients, instructing them, hearing some of their stories, Mick realized that he, too, was a people person. He was good at engineering and it fit his personality and abilities, but he used his skills to work only with objects. Most days he hardly spoke with anyone. He began to think dentistry might be a good job for him because it would allow him to use his head (for critical thinking and design), his hands (in skilled workmanship), and his heart (interacting with and helping people).

At that point, Mick was thirty-three with a wife and two young children. Becoming a dentist would not be easy. Before he could even apply for dental school, he had to return to college to take some science courses that had not been required for his engineering degree. While he went to school, he worked part time, making dentures. Seven years and some loans later, Mick Reynolds graduated with a degree in dentistry and entered a profession he truly enjoyed.

Dr. Reynolds is not the only person who enjoys being a dentist. Every year *U.S. News and World Report* rates some of the common occupations of Americans. In 2017, the magazine considered 183 different jobs, looking at salary, advancement opportunities, industry growth, stress level, and job satisfaction. For the third year in a row, "dentist" was ranked as the best job in the country. Two dental specialist jobs also made the top ten: orthodontist and oral and maxillofacial surgeon.

These three jobs are not the only possibilities in the dental career pathway. The field of dentistry has at least four distinct types of positions, and each of these has a variety of options. Dentists can follow one of ten different career paths. Dental hygienists can choose to practice as part of a dental team, on their own, or in a public health clinic. Dental assistants can pursue advanced positions or go into one of the specialty areas. A fourth career path, also with many branches, is that of dental lab technician.

Working in a dental office, clinic, or lab is just one route. The dental careers pathway can also lead to jobs in research, teaching, and business and management. Whatever the path, whatever the level, whatever the setting, a career in dentistry is interesting, challenging, and very fulfilling.

chapter 1

Dentist: Doctor of Oral Health

People often think of dentists as tooth doctors. Yes, dentists "fix" teeth that are hurting, but they do far more. Dentists are medical doctors who are experts in oral health. Oral health is about the well-being of the oral cavity—the mouth. The oral cavity involves not only teeth, but also the gums, the tongue, and the bones of the jaw and face. These structures control or affect a number of important functions. The World Dental Federation defines oral health as "the ability to speak, smile, taste, touch, chew, swallow, and convey a range of emotions through facial expressions with confidence and without pain, discomfort, and disease." General dentists are concerned with all aspects of oral health—diagnosis, treatment, and prevention of problems.

Spotting Problems

The diagnosis part of dentists' work begins when they look in their patients' mouths. Dentists use a small mirror to see behind and between the teeth and a metal probe to feel the teeth. They check for indications of tooth decay and for any softening of enamel, the tooth's outer coating. They can see if there are any teeth that are cracked or worn down. Dentists also examine the gums. Swelling or redness of the gums may mean the patient

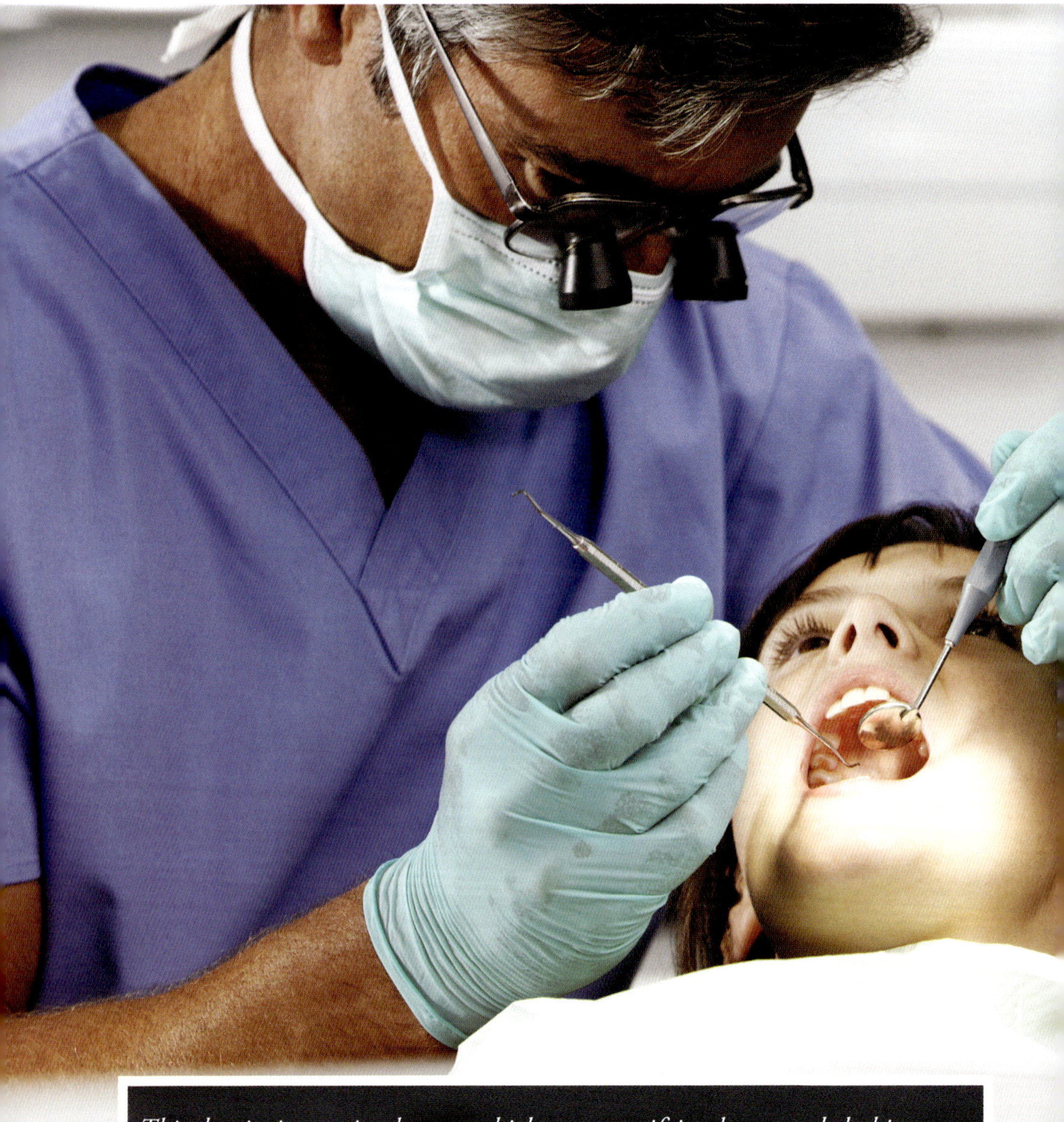

This dentist is wearing loupes, which are magnifying lenses, to help him see small details of a patient's teeth. He is also using a dental probe and mirror.

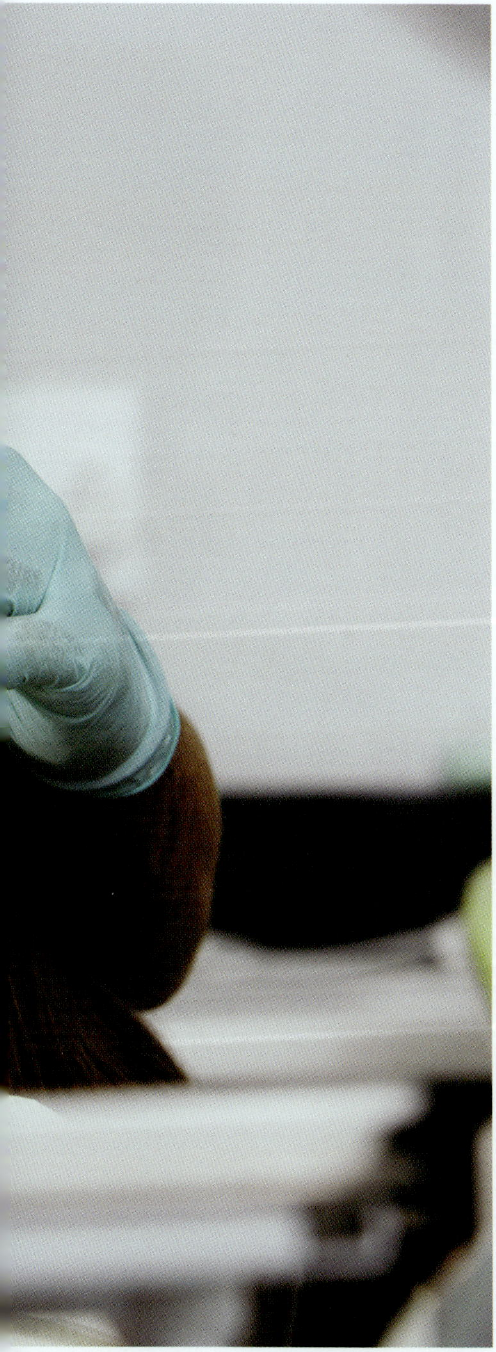

has an infection, a vitamin deficiency, a gum disease, or a more serious condition. Pale gums can be a sign of anemia. Dentists have sometimes diagnosed patients as having diabetes primarily by inspecting their gums.

Teeth and gums are only the beginning of the diagnostic exam. Dentists must evaluate the condition of the tongue and the soft tissues inside the mouth. These can reveal signs of infection or disease. They also examine the patient's bite, or how the upper and lower teeth come together. This alignment is important not only for appearance, but also for speaking, chewing, and keeping teeth clean. A bite that is not aligned properly can cause jaw pain. Dentists feel their patients' necks under and behind the jaws for lumps that might suggest a medical problem such as thyroid or oral cancer.

In addition to performing a detailed visual inspection, dentists use X-rays to examine what they cannot see with their eyes alone. The X-rays, also called radiographs, can detect decay in hidden spots between teeth. They can reveal tiny fractures and show problems in the bone below the gumline. Radiographs expose impacted teeth, teeth that are blocked from breaking through the gums as they should. They also show abscesses, cysts and tumors, and sinus problems. If any of these conditions are left untreated, the result can be major illness or pain.

TREATING PROBLEMS

The goal of dental treatment is not simply to remove pain and prevent disease; it is also to keep the mouth healthy and looking nice. In the past, when people had toothaches, dentists often pulled out the offending tooth. Today, dentists try to fix the tooth so it looks and functions as it did before the problem occurred. When they discover a decaying tooth, they remove the decay and fill the cavity, keeping the tooth intact.

The teeth cannot always be saved. Sometimes they are so badly broken or decayed or fit so poorly they have to be removed. In these cases, treatment includes restoration, which means bringing back what used to be there. After treating the problem, dentists restore the appearance and function of individual teeth by covering them with crowns. They use bridges to fill in spaces where teeth are missing and dentures to replace all or several teeth.

PREVENTING PROBLEMS

In addition to treating dental conditions and restoring healthy smiles, dentists help patients prevent situations that would require treatment or restoration. One preventive measure is the application of fluoride and sealants to the teeth of children and adolescents. Fluoride is a mineral that strengthens teeth. A sealant is a protective cover. The tops of the molars—that is, the chewing surfaces of the back teeth—often develop pits and very tiny crevices. Dentists can minimize the possibility of this type of damage by coating the molars with a thin layer of material, usually plastic. The sealant fills in any chinks and cracks and keeps more from forming.

Dental treatments such as filling cavities also serve to prevent future problems. However, the treatment itself can present some difficulties, and dentists have to be prepared for those. They usually administer anesthetics to prevent patients from feeling pain during a procedure. Sometimes they give sedatives to help nervous or fearful patients relax. They may need to prescribe antibiotics or pain medication to keep patients from getting an infection or suffering pain after a procedure. Patients can be allergic or particularly sensitive to items the dentist typically uses, and the dentist has to make adjustments for

Looks Matter

Sometimes teeth may be perfectly healthy but not very attractive. Teeth may be crooked, unusually shaped, or spaced too close together or too far apart. Some may be too long or too short. They may be discolored. Dentists can adjust these flaws. Improving the appearance of teeth is called cosmetic treatment (for the sake of looks) rather than therapeutic treatment (for the sake of curing). General dentists provide a number of cosmetic services. They bleach teeth to make them whiter. They contour teeth that are irregular, sculpting them to a more desirable shape by sanding away bits of enamel. If one or two teeth are worn down, chipped, or unusually small, or if a gap between teeth is too large, the dentist builds up the teeth by bonding a resin material to them. When the surfaces of front teeth are uneven or greatly discolored, a dentist may cement thin porcelain or plastic veneers to them. Cosmetic dentistry may not affect people's oral health, but it can make a big difference in how they feel about themselves.

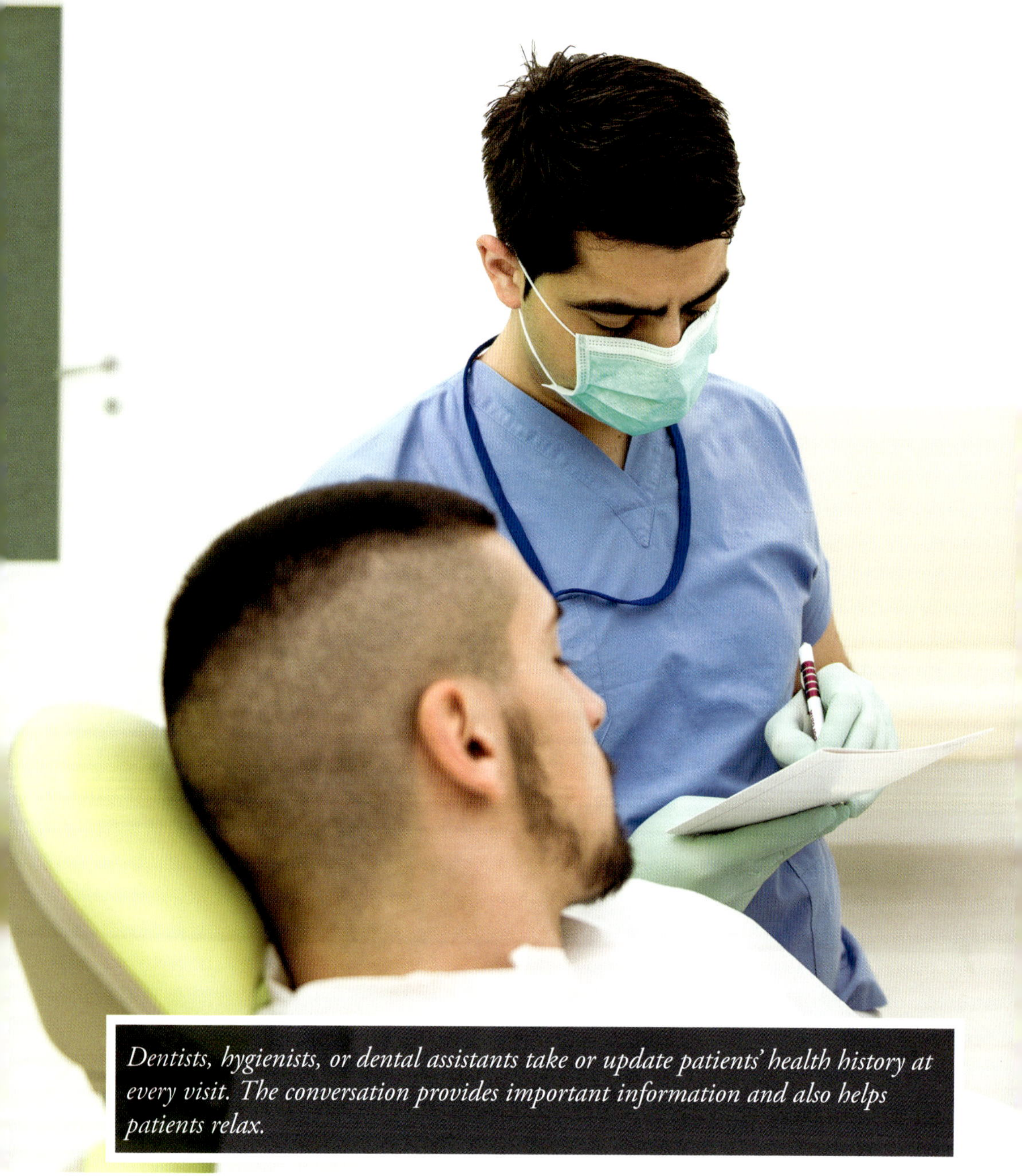

Dentists, hygienists, or dental assistants take or update patients' health history at every visit. The conversation provides important information and also helps patients relax.

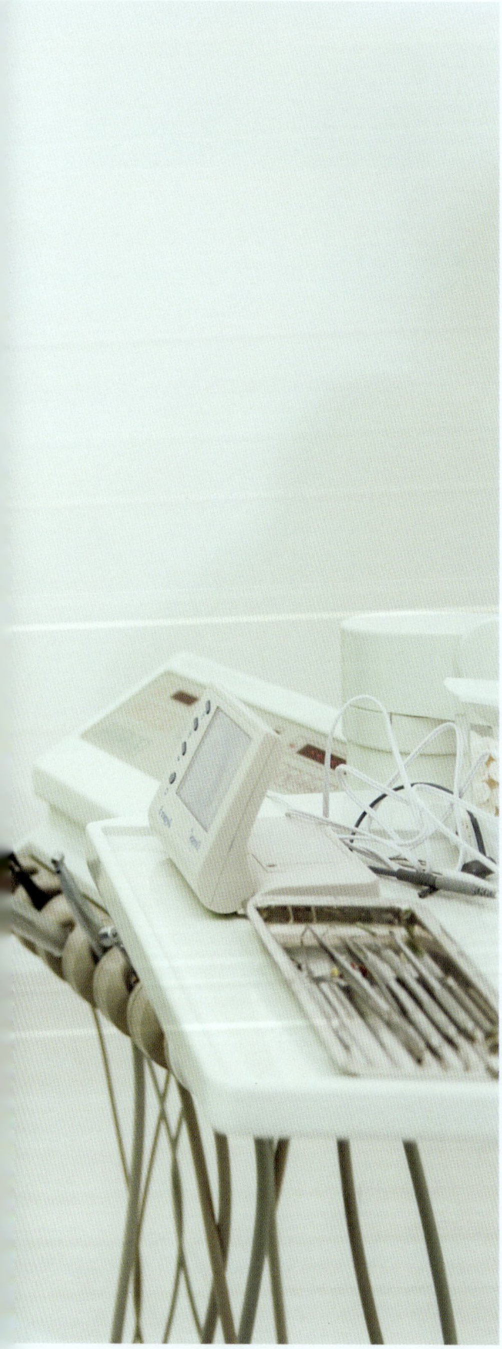

them. Dentists must be knowledgeable about many types of medications.

Dental Specialties

Eighty percent of dentists are general dentists. They handle the oral health issues most people encounter. However, some situations and some patients require more than a general dentist is able to provide. For those cases, the dentistry career path offers nine more branches, or nine different dental specialties.

A dentist who specializes in treating children is a pediatric dentist. Pediatric dentists are much like general dentists, but they limit their practice to children, from infants to adolescents. Many children, as well as some adults, also see orthodontists. Orthodontists help people have proper bites. They use braces and appliances, or devices, to straighten teeth so the upper and lower teeth line up correctly.

The dentistry specialty that focuses on the gums and the bones that support the teeth is

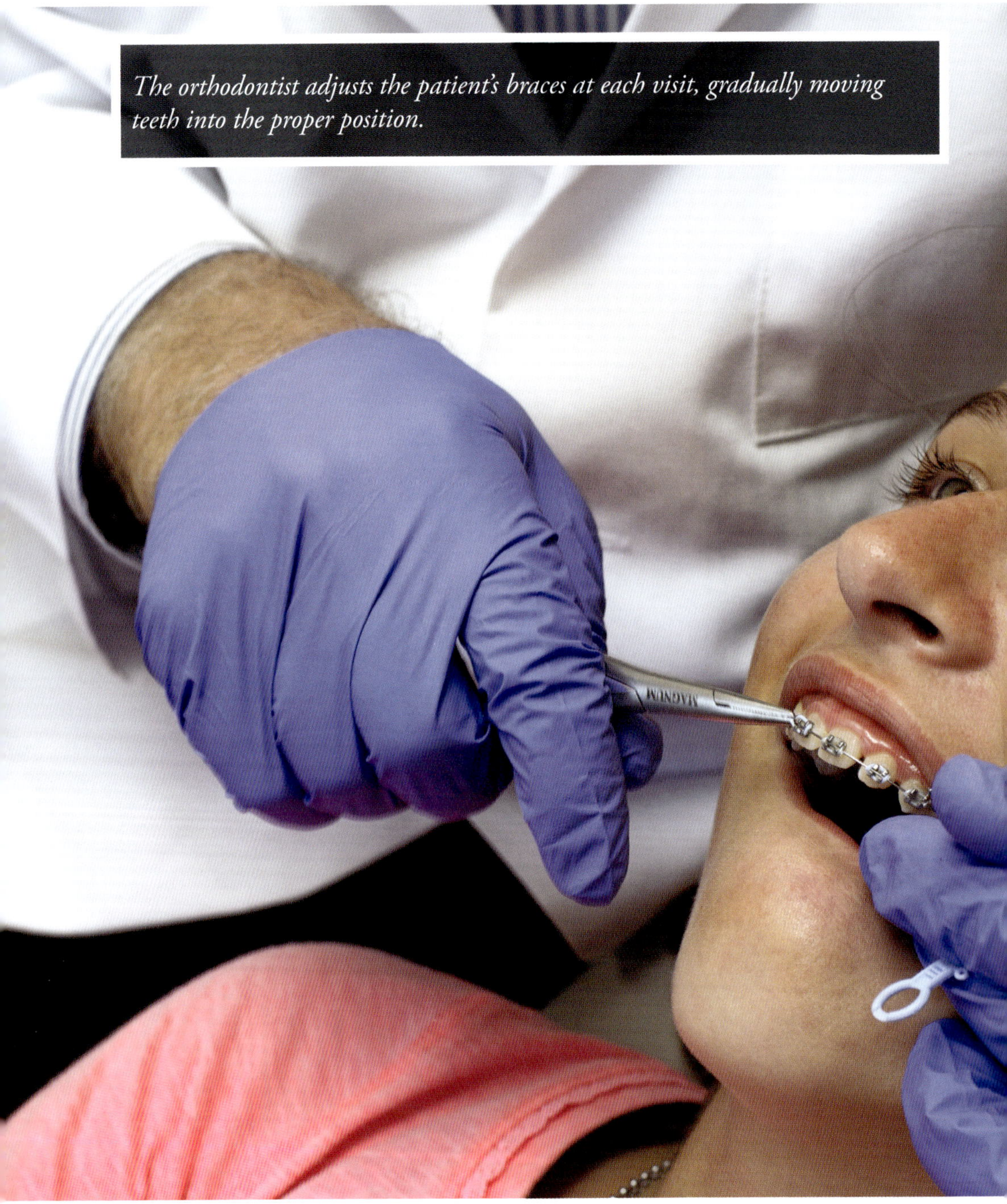

The orthodontist adjusts the patient's braces at each visit, gradually moving teeth into the proper position.

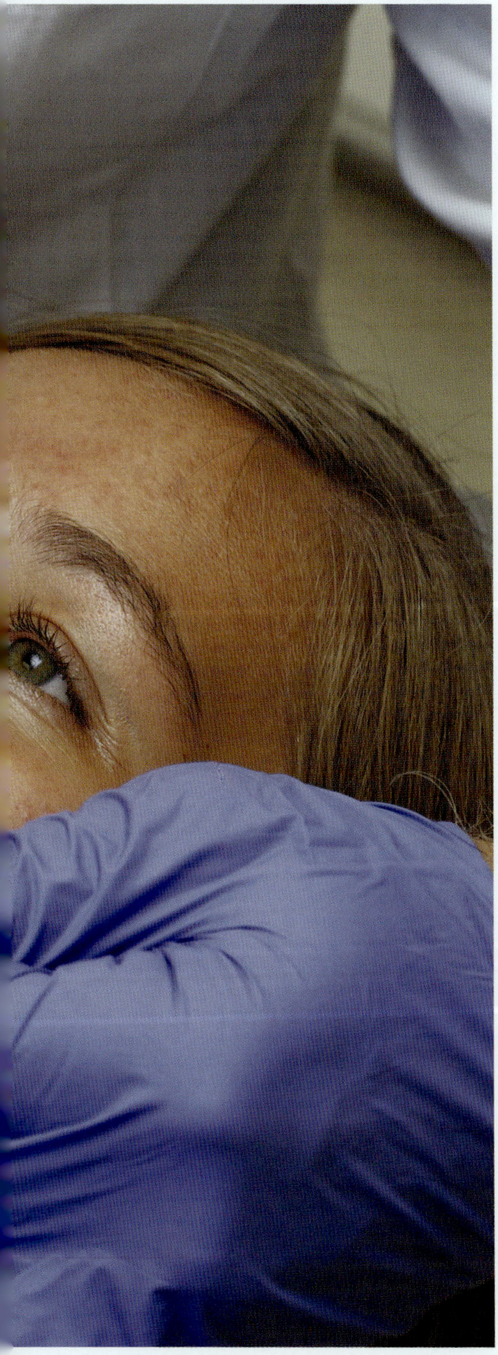

periodontics ("peri-" means "around" and "odont" means "tooth"). Periodontists treat gum disease. Because they have specific training in bones and gums, periodontists can install dental implants, replacement teeth mounted to posts that are inserted into the jawbone.

Some dentists study the insides of the tooth, the pulp and other soft tissue underneath the enamel. They are endodontists ("endo-" means "inside"). They are experts in performing root canals and are usually called on to save teeth that have been badly injured.

When teeth cannot be saved, a prosthodontist may be needed. Prosthodontics is the specialty concerned with restoring or replacing missing teeth ("prostho-" means "replacement"). Prosthodontists make and insert crowns, bridges, dentures, and implants. Other dentists can also perform these tasks, but the more difficult cases are generally referred to these specialists.

Three dental specialties involve diseases, disorders, and injuries of the mouth, jaws, and face. These are the oral and maxillofacial specialties. Oral and maxillofacial pathologists diagnose diseases in these areas, radiologists produce and explain X-ray-type images of these conditions, and surgeons treat the conditions.

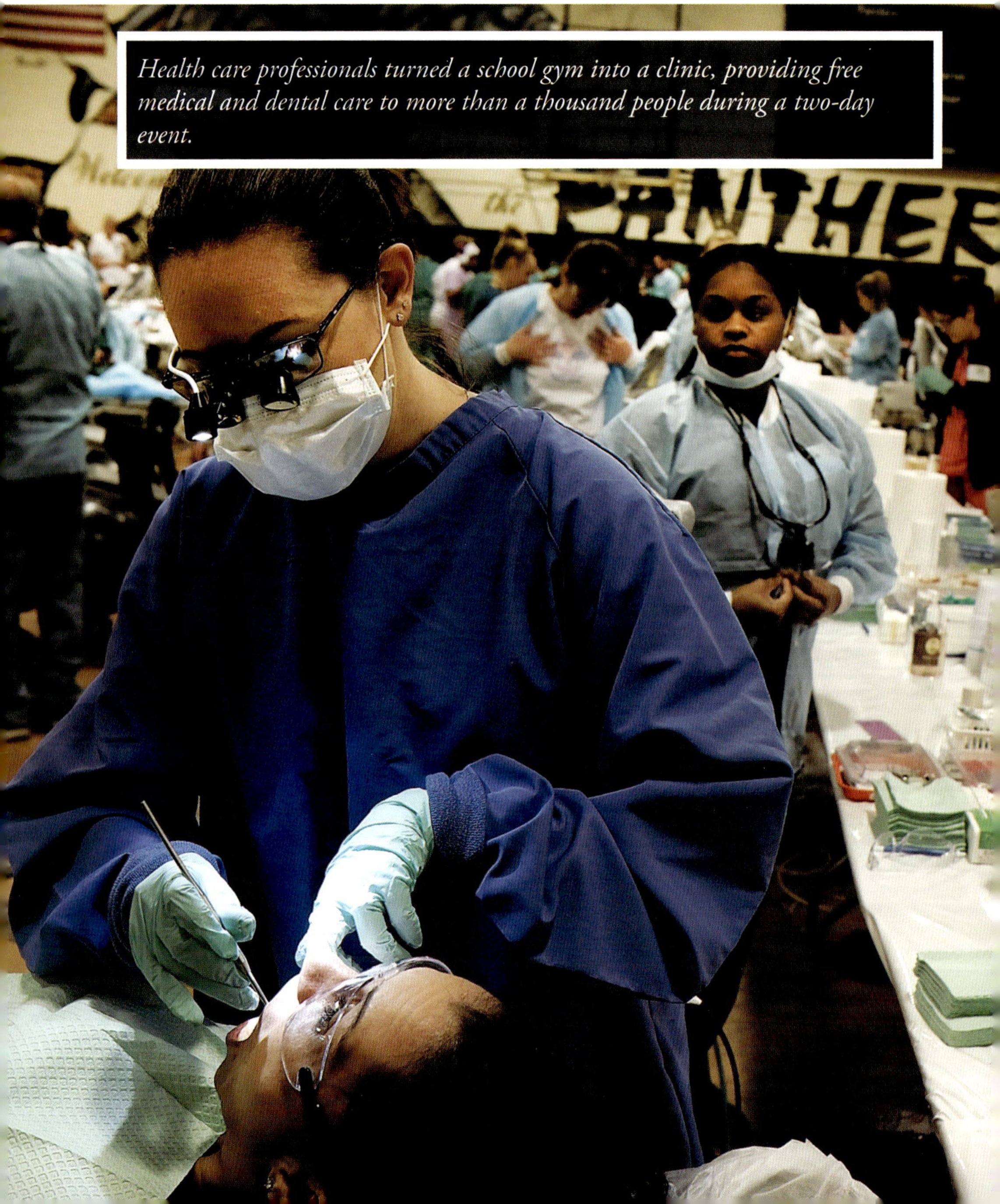

Health care professionals turned a school gym into a clinic, providing free medical and dental care to more than a thousand people during a two-day event.

The ninth specialty is dental public health. Public health dentists are something like general dentists for a community. They are not concerned with individual patients or specific types of dentistry; their focus is the oral health of an entire community. They coordinate the efforts of several groups, such as clinics, dental associations, schools, private agencies, and other health care professionals, to address prevention and control of dental problems in the community.

Why and How to Become a Dentist

Any one of the ten different career possibilities for a dentist—general dentistry or one of the nine specialties—is a great choice. Dentistry is a highly respected profession with a very good income. Many dentists own their own practices, so they are also business professionals. While some people in health care work long and late hours, dentists generally have regular schedules with a decent amount of time off. Their work does not usually involve life and death decisions, so it is less stressful than other jobs in the medical field. Perhaps the biggest plus of a career in dentistry is that dentists genuinely help people; their reward is often, literally, a big smile.

Becoming a dentist requires a lot of education—college followed by at least four years of dental school. Almost all dental schools want students to have a bachelor's degree, but entrance requirements differ by school. Some college courses in biology and chemistry are nearly always required, and some schools require a science degree. To be eligible for dental school, students must pass the Dental Admission Test.

In a dental school accredited by the American Dental Association, students study microbiology, anatomy, nutrition, oral health and surgery, and similar subjects. They get hands-on practice in all kinds of dental techniques and procedures. When they graduate, they are awarded a degree that goes by one of three names: doctor of dental surgery (DDS), doctor of dental medicine (DDM), or doctor of medical dentistry (DMD). If they want to practice in one of the dental specialties, they need two to four additional years of study and practice.

Having a degree is not enough to begin practicing dentistry. A dentist must also have a license. Licenses are given by states. Every state requires that candidates for a license pass both a written test and a clinical test to demonstrate their knowledge and skills. Most states use the tests of the American Dental Association as a basis for licensing.

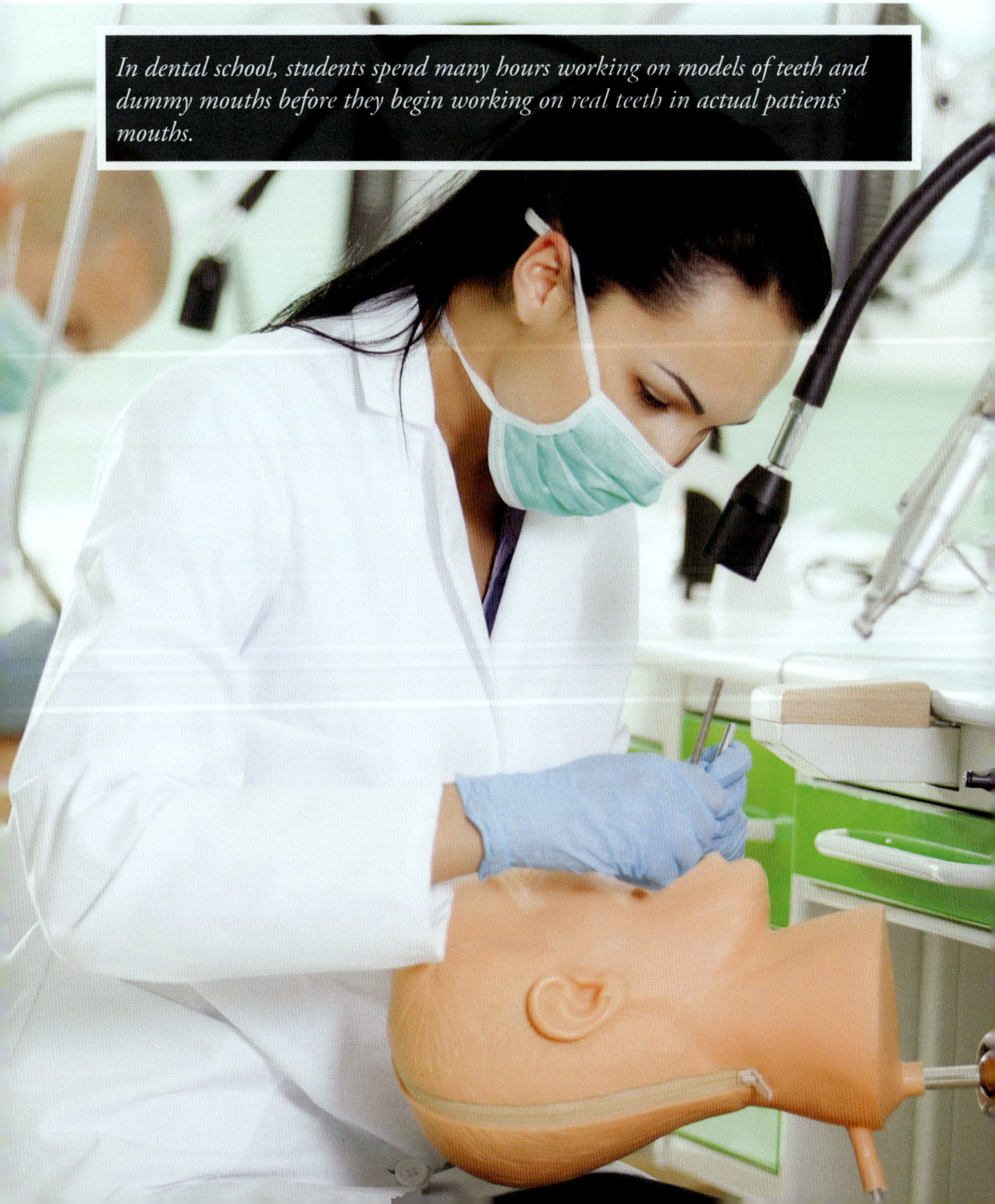

In dental school, students spend many hours working on models of teeth and dummy mouths before they begin working on real teeth in actual patients' mouths.

Some people who want to become dentists hesitate because dental school is so expensive; a four-year program can cost between $138,000 and $234,000. That is a lot of money, but getting it is not impossible. On their websites, the American Student Dental Association and the American Dental Education Association list and provide links to a number of grants, scholarships, and loans that are available. The organizations also have tips for applying for financial help.

One way of funding a dental school education is through military service. A US Army health professions scholarship program pays tuition and gives a stipend that enables people to complete dental school at no cost in return for serving a period of time in the army. Other military branches have similar programs. For students who amass large school loans, there are resources that help with loan repayment. Some national and state government programs will pay part of the loan amount for dentists who agree to work for a few years in an area or a clinic where dentists are in short supply.

If the thought of so much schooling and so much money is intimidating, remember these two things: First, the high salary dentists can expect to earn is usually enough to pay even a large debt fairly quickly. Second, nearly every dentist who has paid the cost of dental school has said the struggle was well worth the effort; they love their jobs!

chapter 2

Dental Hygienist: Prevention Specialist

The dentist is the expert in treating dental problems, but dentists have partners when it comes to prevention. That partner is the dental hygienist. The primary job of dental hygienists is to keep their patients from developing problems in their mouths. Dental hygienists are the prevention specialists of oral health care.

Because "hygiene" means "clean," people sometimes think dental hygienists merely clean teeth. They may not realize that cleaning teeth is the main way of preventing cavities, diseases, toothaches, and other problems. Most dental issues begin with plaque. Plaque is a thin film made up of tiny bits of food, dead cells from tissues inside the mouth, and bacteria. It is sticky and attaches itself to the teeth. The bacteria in the plaque produce acids that eat into the enamel, the hard, outside layer of the teeth. This action is how cavities are formed. The plaque also produces toxins, or poisons, that can damage the gums. Thus, cleaning teeth is necessary to prevent tooth decay and gum disease.

Cleanliness Equals Prevention

Plaque is soft and is easily removed by proper, thorough brushing and flossing. However, if plaque is allowed to stay on the teeth for longer than twenty-four hours, it hardens. The hardened plaque, called tartar or calculus, is rough and porous. It contains many microscopic openings where more plaque with more bacteria can stick. Tartar cannot be brushed or flossed away; it must be scraped off. This task is a job for the dental hygienist.

Cleaning teeth is not as easy as it may sound. Hygienists have to remove the tartar without damaging the tooth enamel. They use a variety of scalers, instruments with small, triangular blades. The blades are different sizes and curved at different angles so the hygienist can reach all the parts of all the teeth in different positions in the mouth. To clean the part of the tooth below the gumline, they switch to curettes, scalers with rounded tips. Sometimes they also use ultrasonic scalers, instruments that vibrate to loosen up the tartar. They have to decide which tool is best for each situation, and they typically use several for the same patient.

A tooth cleaning always ends with a polish. Like the

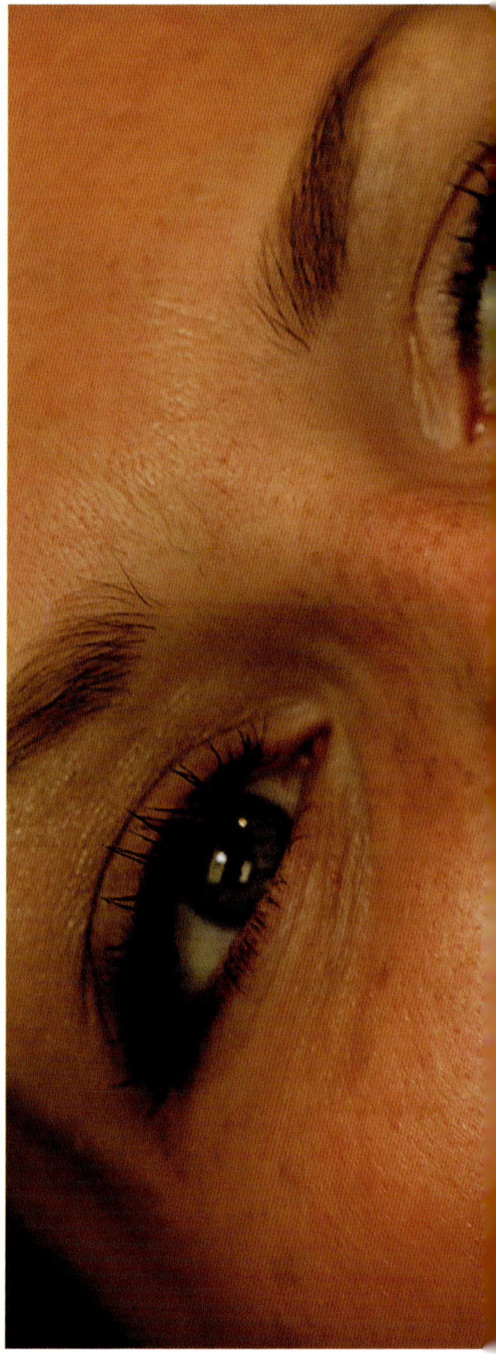

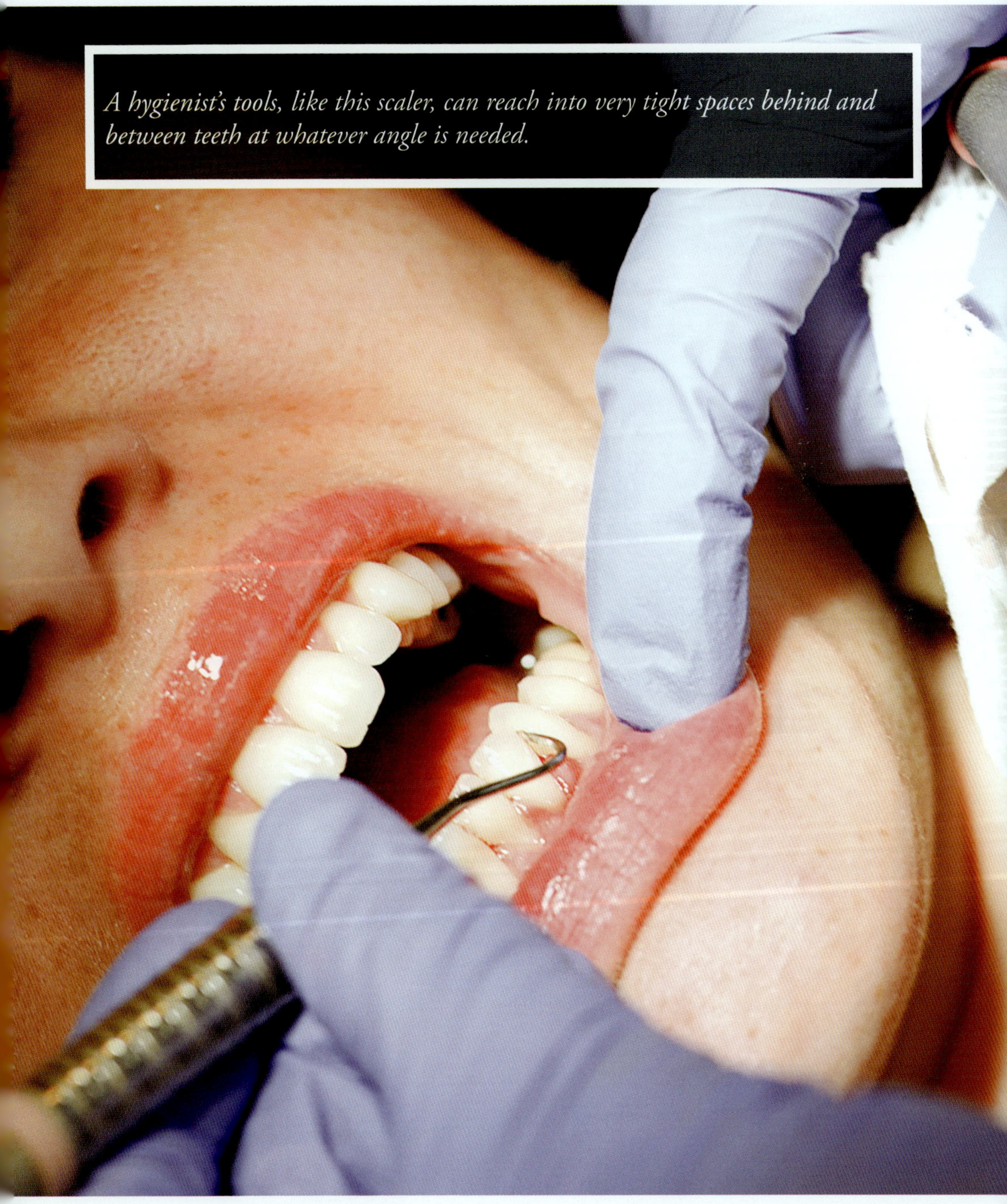

A hygienist's tools, like this scaler, can reach into very tight spaces behind and between teeth at whatever angle is needed.

cleaning, polishing is a preventive measure. The purpose of the polish is not to make the teeth gleam; it is to make them smooth. Plaque forms every day, and plaque sticks to a rough surface more easily than to something smooth. The hygienist sends the patient home with a healthy mouth that is resistant to plaque buildup.

PREVENTION REQUIRES KNOWLEDGE

Tooth cleaning is the primary work of hygienists, but their job of preventing dental problems begins the minute the patient sits in the chair. The hygienist is usually the person in the office who records patients' health histories and takes their blood pressure and pulse. These actions are important in detecting and preventing problems during treatment.

For example, when dentists and hygienists work with sharp instruments, they may poke a patient's gums, releasing bacteria in the mouth into the bloodstream. In patients with certain medical conditions, having that bacteria in the blood can be very dangerous. When hygienists learn a patient has one of these conditions, they

can give that patient antibiotics before treatment to prevent the possibility of infection. Medical situations can change, so dental hygienists update patient information at every visit. Sometimes in the course of asking questions and taking blood

Blood pressure is sometimes measured with a device placed on the wrist or on the finger. This dental hygienist is using the traditional blood pressure cuff.

pressure measurements, hygienists spot signs that concern them. They alert the patient to their concern and suggest the patient consult a medical doctor. Dental hygienists have prevented problems that go beyond oral health!

After the overall health evaluation, hygienists examine the patient's mouth and teeth as well as the jaw and neck. They check the teeth for soft spots that indicate decay and see how healthy the gums are. They take radiographs so they can find cavities they may miss otherwise. In most states, hygienists are not allowed to diagnose diseases, but they usually are able to recognize them, and they refer patients who need more than preventive care to a dentist for treatment.

Prevention Means Education

The greatest preventive service a dentist or hygienist can perform is to teach patients what they can do to maintain their own oral health. Hygienists demonstrate how to brush and floss properly. They show patients different kinds of toothbrushes and various tools they can use to keep their teeth free of plaque and tartar. They explain the benefits of pastes, gels, and mouthwashes and make recommendations based on individual needs. Hygienists talk with their patients about the things they put in their mouths—food, chewing gum, cigarettes—and how they affect their teeth. They work with patients to develop and focus on individualized dental hygiene care plans. The plan details what the patient needs to do at home, what the hygienist will do at the next visit, and when that appointment will be.

Beyond Prevention

What hygienists can do depends on the states in which they practice. In some states, they are limited to evaluating patients, cleaning their teeth, and providing education. However, a trend

Dental Hygienists Save Lives

On January 11, 2007, Deamonte Driver complained of a headache. The doctor told Deamonte's mother that the twelve-year-old had a dental abscess, an infection around the root of a tooth. The doctor gave him medicine, but the infection had spread from his tooth to his brain. Within days, he was rushed to a hospital, where he underwent two brain surgeries and treatment for seizures. However, the medical attention was too late; on February 25, Deamonte died. Basically, he died because of an untreated cavity.

Contrast Deamonte's story with that of eleven-year-old Journee Woodard. Unlike Deamonte, Journee went to the dentist regularly. On one visit, her hygienist noticed something amiss. Not with her teeth; with her eyes. Dental hygienists are trained to observe their patients thoroughly, and the hygienist thought Journee's eyes looked a little yellow. Recognizing yellow eyes as a possible sign of an internal problem, the hygienist and the dentist urged Journee's mother to take her to her family doctor immediately. Within a week, doctors removed a tumor as big as a grapefruit from Journee's pancreas. The tumor would have eventually ruptured, causing major damage and probable death. Neither Journee nor her parents had any idea that something was dangerously wrong, but an alert dental hygienist did. That hygienist is the Woodard family's hero!

has been growing for hygienists to be permitted to perform some of the tasks usually done only by dentists. The reason for this is that the number of dentists in the United States is not keeping up with the need. Several states allow hygienists with proper training to apply sealants and fluorides, administer anesthetics, put in temporary fillings, and assist in oral surgery.

A dental hygienist helps a patient learn how to hold floss and position her hands so she can floss her teeth properly.

Traditionally dental hygienists have worked in dental offices under the supervision of dentists. States, however, are beginning to allow hygienists with advanced training to set up their own practices. These hygienists are given special licenses and job titles such as "registered dental hygienist in alternative practice" or "advanced dental therapist." Although they work independently and can perform some of the tasks of dentists, they usually have to have a professional relationship with a dentist so they can refer patients who need treatment they cannot provide.

Dental professionals recognize the value of a hygienist who can administer some treatment as well as prevention. Because of the shortage of dentists, many people do not get the dental care they need. The situation is especially severe in rural and minority communities, where residents often do not have dental insurance, have difficulty getting transportation to a dental office, and may not be able to afford dental care. The American Dental Hygienists' Association came up with a solution: a model for a dental career path for people who would practice in communities that need them. It is called the advanced dental hygiene practitioner model because it allows hygienists to deliver an advanced level of care.

Advanced dental hygiene practitioners are basically a cross between hygienists and dentists. They must be able to do everything a hygienist is expected to do and some things dentists do. They can provide diagnostic and preventive treatment and perform restorative services in underserved communities—places where there are not enough dentists. Instead of working in a dental office, they typically practice in public health clinics, schools, nursing homes, group homes, and hospitals. A number of states are licensing hygienists for advanced practice.

BECOMING A HYGIENIST

Like dentists, hygienists are licensed in the state in which they serve. Each state sets its own standards for obtaining a license, but most follow the national guidelines of the American Dental Association for awarding the registered dental hygienist license. The basic requirement is a two-year course of study from an accredited training program—a school approved by the American Dental Association. In those two years, students spend about 2,300 hours in the classroom. They study general sciences, such as anatomy, physiology, and microbiology. They take classes in radiology, nutrition, and medications. They take courses in dental science, such as periodontics, and they study the anatomy of the mouth, head, neck, and jaw. In addition, they spend about five hundred hours actually practicing the skills they learn. This training is offered at community colleges, technical colleges, and dental schools. Graduates earn either a certificate or an associate's degree.

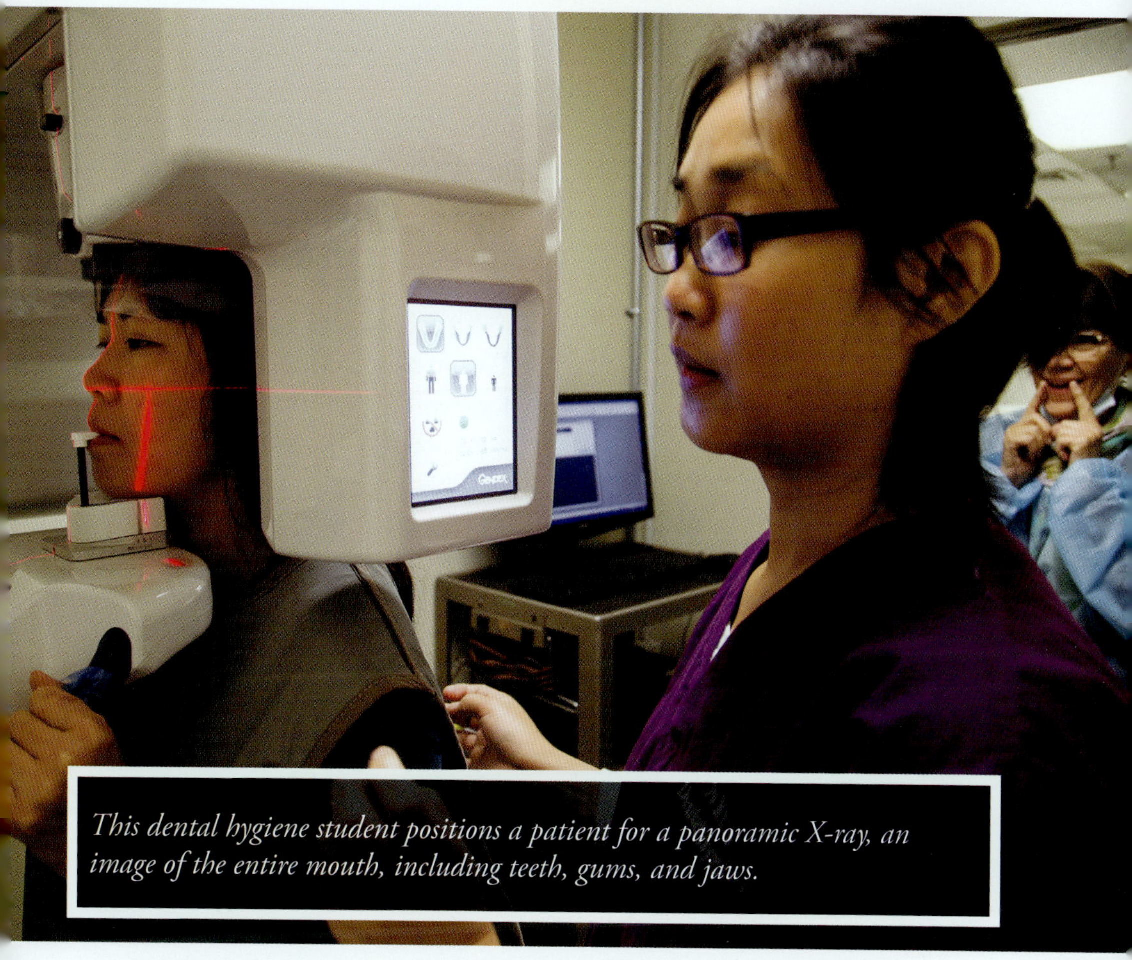

This dental hygiene student positions a patient for a panoramic X-ray, an image of the entire mouth, including teeth, gums, and jaws.

People who want to practice in public health settings rather than in a dental office need a bachelor's degree, which takes four years of education. In the additional two years, students take classes in health education and patient counseling, and they have more hours of clinical practice, which means practice in actually treating people. Colleges and dental schools have four-year programs. Hygienists who want to train other hygienists, manage dental clinics, or do consulting work complete even more schooling, earning a master of science degree in dental hygiene.

For people enrolled in these programs, job prospects are good. According to the United States Department of Labor, the country needs thousands more dental hygienists every year, and the demand is growing. This career path offers high income potential, a short educational requirement for entry-level positions, and great flexibility. Registered dental hygienists can expect to make more money than technicians in most other medical fields, and they can begin earning money after only two years of education. They can find jobs that are full time and jobs that are part time. The American Dental Hygienists' Association lists more than 330 accredited programs that prepare people for this very attractive career.

chapter 3

Dental Assistant: Another Set of Hands

While dentists and hygienists provide the prevention and treatment that make people's mouths look nice and stay healthy, dental assistants are busy behind the scenes, enabling the dentist and hygienist to do their jobs smoothly. They are not simply aides who stand ready to follow whatever a dentist orders them to do. They are essential employees who carry out a wide variety of tasks that make the dental office pleasant, safe, and efficient.

Chairside Assisting

As the term "assistant" implies, the dental assistant helps dentists perform their duties. Assistants have to be familiar with a number of different procedures. They need to know what instruments and materials will be needed, in what order they will be used, and how the particular dentist operates. They provide whatever the dentist needs before, during, and after each procedure.

Before patients arrive, either in the morning or the night before, the dental assistant prepares a tray for each one. The tray holds the implements and supplies the dentist will need to treat the patient. Setting trays up ahead of time, specific for each procedure, is important as a number of items are usually

This dental assistant prepared a tray of dental tools for the dentist to use with one patient. She will be responsible for handing the dentist the right tool at the right time.

needed. The tray for a simple cavity removal and tooth filling contains at least fifteen items!

During the procedure, the assistant hands the items to the dentist at the proper times. This is not as simple as it sounds. Dentists cannot look away from the patient, and they often have to work quickly. Assistants take one instrument from the dentist and give him or her another, using only one hand in one smooth motion. They have to anticipate which tool is next and when the dentist wants it. There is an art to exchanging instruments, and learning that art takes training and practice.

This type of help, in which the assistant sits next to the seated patient, is called chairside assisting. It is generally part of a system known as "four-handed dentistry." In this arrangement, the two hands of the dental assistant help the two hands of the dentist in the treatment of patients. The assistant suctions water, saliva, and debris from patients' mouths and uses an air-water syringe to clean particular areas as the dentist continues to work. The specific clinical tasks a dental assistant can perform are determined by each state. They are limited because the assistant's training and skills are limited. But the help the assistant is permitted to provide is invaluable in enabling dentists to treat patients quickly and efficiently.

TECHNICIAN RESPONSIBILITIES

In addition to chairside help, dental assistants do some of the technical work that is part of dental practice. When patients need crowns, bridges, or appliances—any item that has to be made and put on the teeth or gums—dentists must make sure the item fits properly. To measure for fit, they work with models of the patients' teeth and gums. Often the models are made by the dental assistant. The assistant takes an impression of the patient's teeth and gums using a soft, waxlike substance. The assistant then mixes another material, pours it into the impression, and allows it to harden into a stone model, an exact replica of the patient's teeth.

Dental assistants also make temporary crowns, although the dentist needs to place them on the patients' teeth. Another function the dental assistant performs is taking radiographs. Assistants in both general dentistry and specialties can take and develop the radiographs, but dentists interpret them.

EMPHASIS ON PEOPLE

The dentist is focused on the patient's treatment, but the dental assistant is concerned with the patient's comfort. The assistant is the first person the patient encounters in the office other than the receptionist, so the assistant sets the tone for the patient's experience. As they greet patients and take them to the treatment room, assistants try to observe how the patients feel about their visit. Some people are in pain, and some are apprehensive about

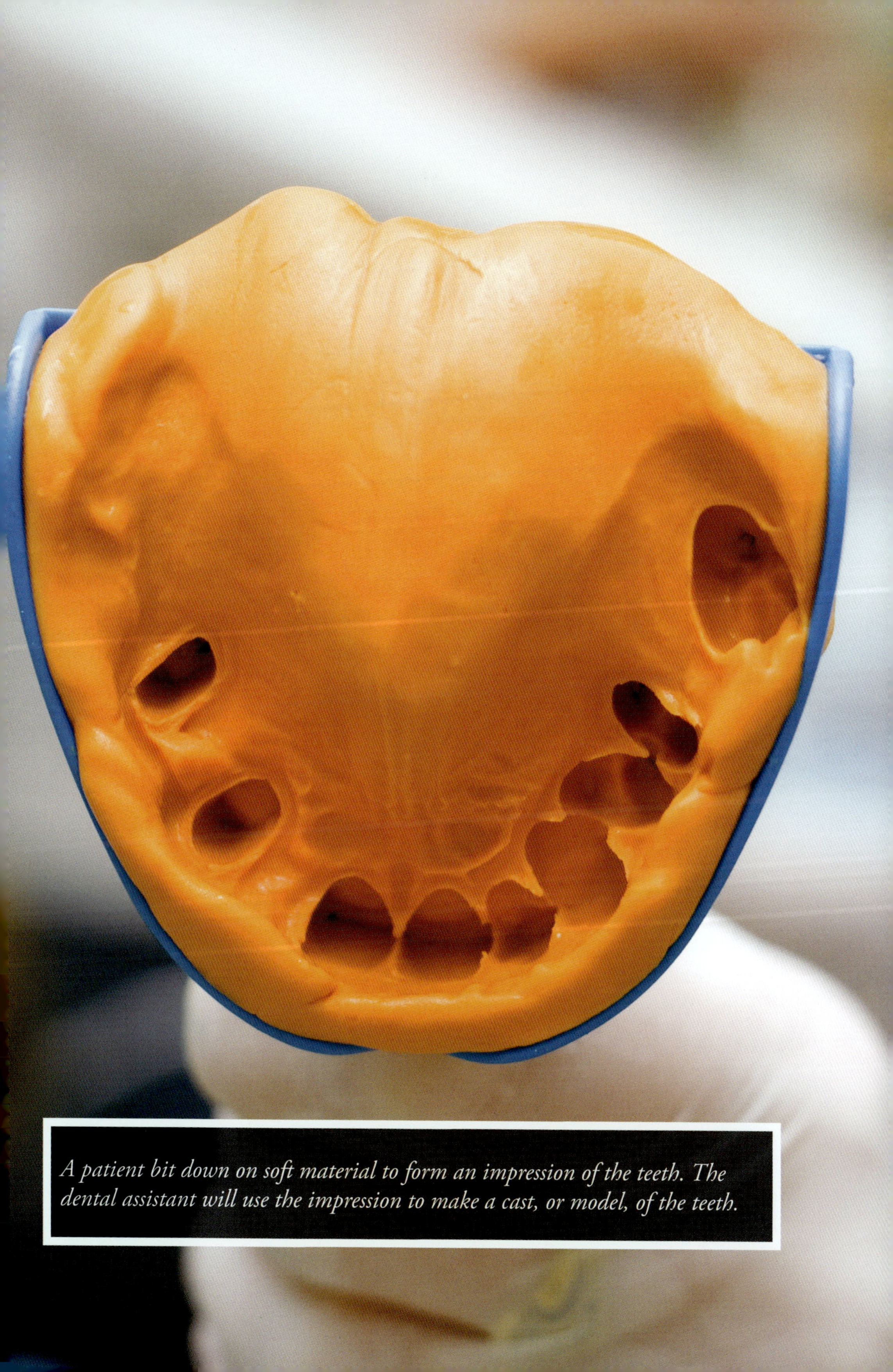

A patient bit down on soft material to form an impression of the teeth. The dental assistant will use the impression to make a cast, or model, of the teeth.

what the dentist will do. Caring, attentive assistants calm patients' fears by explaining what they can expect.

Dental assistants get patients ready for treatment. They review their medical history, including any medications they are taking, and measure their blood pressure and pulse. They record the information in the patients' charts, noting anything that might be useful in making a patient more comfortable at the next visit. After treatment, the assistant documents in the chart everything that is done for the patient.

Dental assistants are also teachers. When the dentist completes the treatment, the assistant explains the next steps. Assistants instruct patients what to do if a temporary comes off, how long to take medications, and when to return for follow-up. They show them how to floss under bridges and teach them to care for their appliances and restorations. Assistants can provide education in all aspects of routine oral health care.

MAINTAINING A SAFE AND EFFICIENT OFFICE

Dental assistants are responsible not only for patients' comfort, but also for their safety. In a medical office, safe means clean. Everything that comes into contact with a patient's mouth, and everything the dentist might touch, must be absolutely clean. Ensuring that is the case is the assistant's job. Before any patient arrives, between patients, and at the end of the day, the dental assistant cleans and disinfects all surfaces in all treatment rooms, including countertops, chairs, equipment, buttons, knobs, and handles. At the end of the day, the assistant sterilizes all the instruments and prepares sterile trays for the next day's procedures.

A safe and efficient office must have all the necessary supplies on hand. The dental assistant is usually the person in charge of keeping track of and ordering supplies. The X-ray machine and lab equipment must be in good order; that, too,

A DENTIST'S PERSPECTIVE

The majority of jobs for dental hygienists and dental assistants are in solo-practice dental offices, businesses owned and managed by one dentist. That means dentists are the ones selecting and hiring the hygienists and assistants. What do they look for in their employees? Of course they want dental skills; people working for and with them have to be able to perform the expected tasks. But they also are interested in qualities that do not necessarily show up on a résumé, difficult-to-measure qualities dentist Gary Eritzian calls the "intangibles."

Dr. Eritzian has practiced dentistry for more than twenty years. In that time, he has interviewed quite a number of hygienists and assistants as well as office staff. He has hired full-time, part-time, and fill-in employees. He has worked with new students and with veterans. With all of them, he looks for a positive attitude, care and respect for others, and a good work ethic. "I can teach someone how to do a procedure," he said in an interview, "but I can't teach cheerfulness or willingness to take on new duties."

How does Dr. Eritzian know if job seekers possess these qualities? He talks with their references. The number one question he asks is "How is their attendance?" He has found that people with good attendance records, who make a practice of being on time, are generally dependable. Dependability is another one of those intangibles that may be the difference between just getting an interview and getting a job.

is the responsibility of the dental assistant. The assistant often functions as the office manager, answering the phone, scheduling appointments, and billing patients. In short, the job of the dental assistant is to manage patients, records, inventory, and treatment rooms as well as work alongside the dentist,

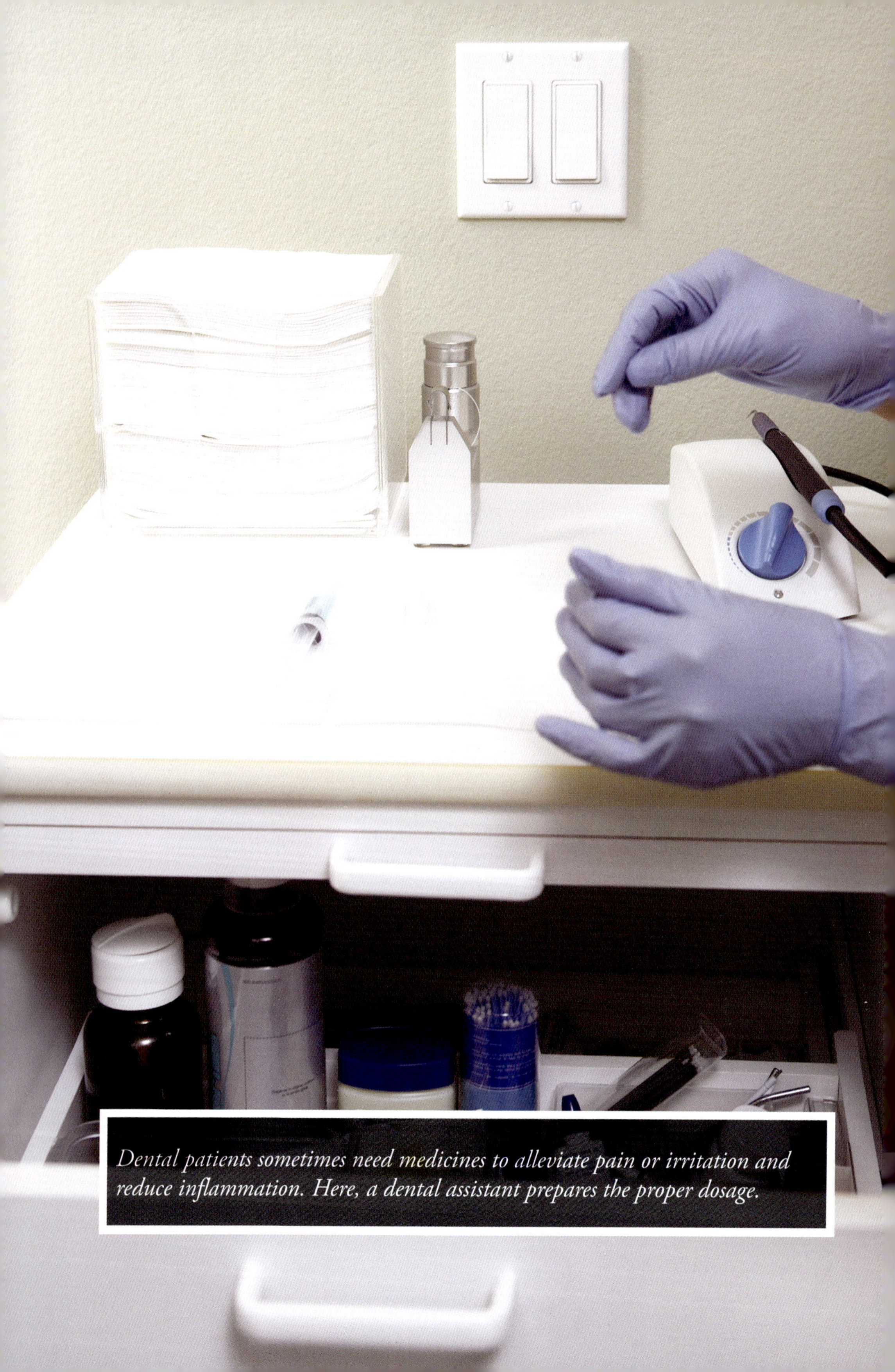

Dental patients sometimes need medicines to alleviate pain or irritation and reduce inflammation. Here, a dental assistant prepares the proper dosage.

participating in whatever direct patient clinical care is permitted by state law.

Beyond the Traditional Role

Although these are the typical duties of the dental assistant, the shortage of dentists is creating new opportunities for dental assistants just as it is for hygienists. There are tasks a dental assistant might be able to do with a little extra training; these tasks are called "enhanced functions." It is up to each state whether an assistant is allowed to perform any of these enhanced functions; each state specifies the functions an assistant is permitted to perform and what training and certification is required before permission is granted. In every state, these functions can be performed only under a dentist's supervision.

The enhanced functions are tasks that are reversible. In other words, an assistant may not do anything that has a permanent effect on the patient's teeth or gums. For example, some states allow an assistant to place or remove temporary fillings, but the assistant cannot drill on the tooth receiving the filling. An assistant may not scale teeth to remove tartar, but after the dentist or hygienist has done the scaling, the assistant may polish the teeth. Other enhanced functions are placing or removing temporary crowns and applying fluoride and sealants.

Becoming a Dental Assistant

Performing these functions obviously takes skill and training. However, the education to enter the career path of dental assistant is far less than for a dentist or a hygienist. In some states, no education beyond high school is necessary; dental assistants can learn on the job. Some high schools offer work-study programs that enable students to learn and acquire skills as they work in some aspects of

The final procedure of many dental visits is polishing the teeth. Polishing leaves a clean feel and look and retards the formation of plaque.

dental assisting, such as sterilizing instruments and preparing exam rooms.

However, many dentists do prefer to hire trained assistants. Training programs can usually be completed in a year or less. Some training institutions offer accelerated courses, part-time classes, and distance education, or study over the internet. Training is available through community colleges, technical and vocational schools, universities, and dental schools. Some of the schools are accredited by the American Dental Association. The basic curriculum generally includes courses in dental science, dental materials and procedures, radiography, infection control, and office management. Courses in the various enhanced functions are also available. Practicing dental assistants can take additional classes to advance their careers. The schools award certificates that confirm that the students have successfully completed the training program.

The Dental Assisting National Board issues certificates that certify that a person is knowledgeable, skilled, and competent in dental assisting. Anyone graduating from an accredited program is eligible to take the test for certification, and someone who has not graduated from an accredited program may take the test after working two years as a dental assistant. The board offers four certifications: certified dental assistant, certified orthodontic assistant, certified preventive functions dental assistant, and certified restorative functions dental assistant. The certifications show what a person is able to do, but the state may still limit what that person is allowed to do.

The trend in dentistry appears to be to permit people to assume more responsibilities as they grow in experience and education. Someone can begin as a dental assistant with very little training, take classes and acquire new skills, and move up in responsibilities and pay. With a little more school, dental assistants can easily move into the role of hygienists. With a lot more school, they can become dentists. Those who choose to remain as dental assistants earn a good wage, generally more than people in other health care support roles. They enjoy the flexibility of working full time or part time and the stimulation of performing a great variety of tasks. And they have the satisfaction of knowing that they provide an essential service that brightens people's lives.

chapter 4

Dental Lab Technician: Scientist and Artist

Dentists, hygienists, and dental assistants work with people; dental lab technicians work with things. Dentists decide what items a patient needs, and lab techs make those items. Thus lab technicians are essential members of the dental health care team. They are scientists; they design and manufacture devices that improve patients' oral health. They are also artists; they shape those devices in such a way that patients look good. Dental lab technicians are needed primarily in two areas of dentistry: restoration and orthodontics.

Prostheses and Appliances

Restorative dentistry involves the repair or replacement of teeth that are broken, chipped, discolored, or missing. The repair is made by substituting an artificial item, or prosthesis, for the damaged or missing parts. Crowns, bridges, veneers, dentures, and implants are dental prostheses.

Orthodontists correct poor bites or improper alignments by moving or stabilizing teeth. They do not need prostheses; they use appliances. An appliance is a device, or a piece of equipment, that serves a particular purpose. A dental appliance serves the purpose of straightening teeth. Common orthodontic

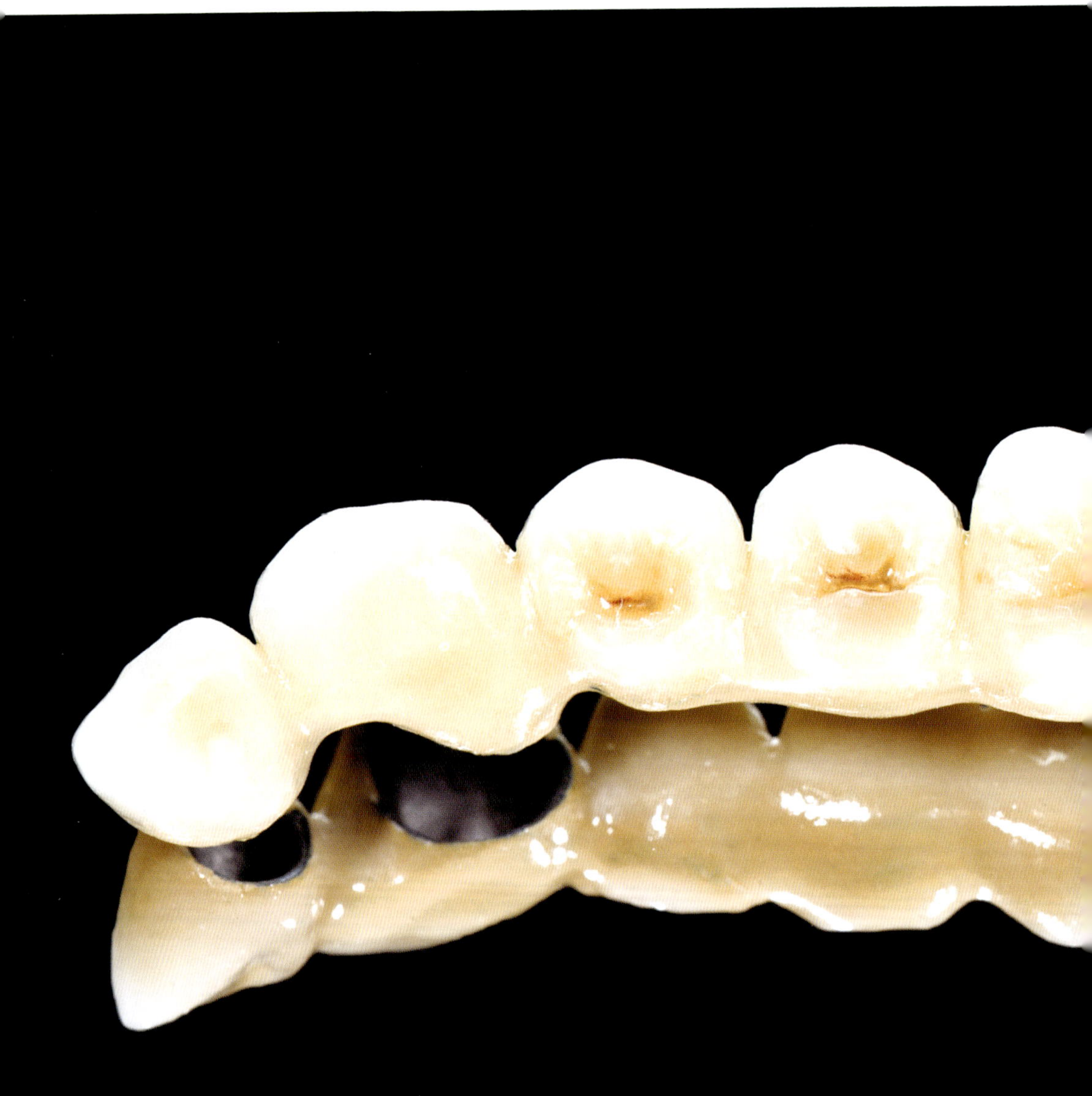

This ceramic bridge will be anchored on three teeth and span the spaces where three teeth are missing.

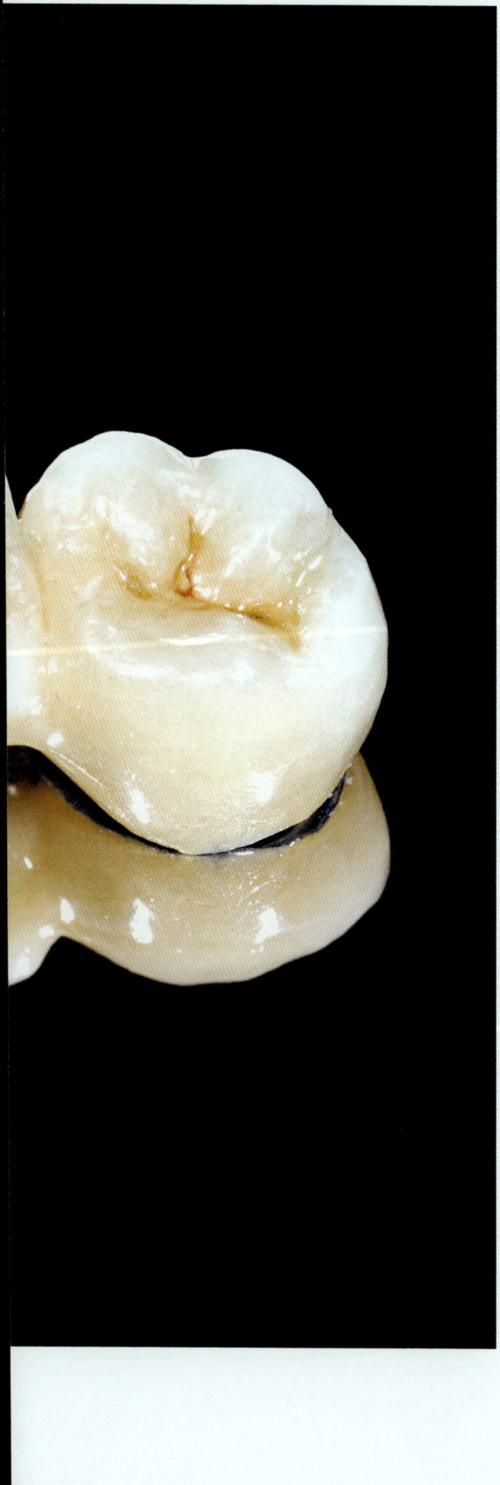

appliances include braces, retainers, expanders, arches, and bite plates.

Each prosthesis and each appliance is a unique item, fitted to the specific needs of an individual patient. Therefore, the technician who makes the restoration or corrective device must work closely with the dentist who orders it. The dentist gives the technician an impression of the patient's teeth and gums and a prescription explaining exactly what the prosthesis or appliance should be like and what it will need to do. The technician creates the item, paying attention to fit, function, and form. The item must sit comfortably in the patient's mouth (fit), work the way natural teeth should (function), and look nice (form).

Science and Art

Getting the proper fit and function is the science part of the job. The technician has to understand tooth anatomy and how all the structures of the mouth work together. Using the impression received from the dentist, the technician makes a model of the patient's teeth. Following the dentist's prescription, the technician designs the prosthesis or appliance that will fit on the model and meet all the physical requirements the dentist specified.

Technicians must know some chemistry and physics. Prostheses and appliances can be made from a variety of different items, each with its own advantages and disadvantages. Technicians have to choose the materials that are best for the particular patient's needs. Should a crown or a bridge be made of porcelain, metal, or a combination of both? Should braces be stainless steel, ceramic, or plastic? Which type of ceramic is best? White comes in many shades; what color tint should the item have? The answers to these and other questions are different for different patients.

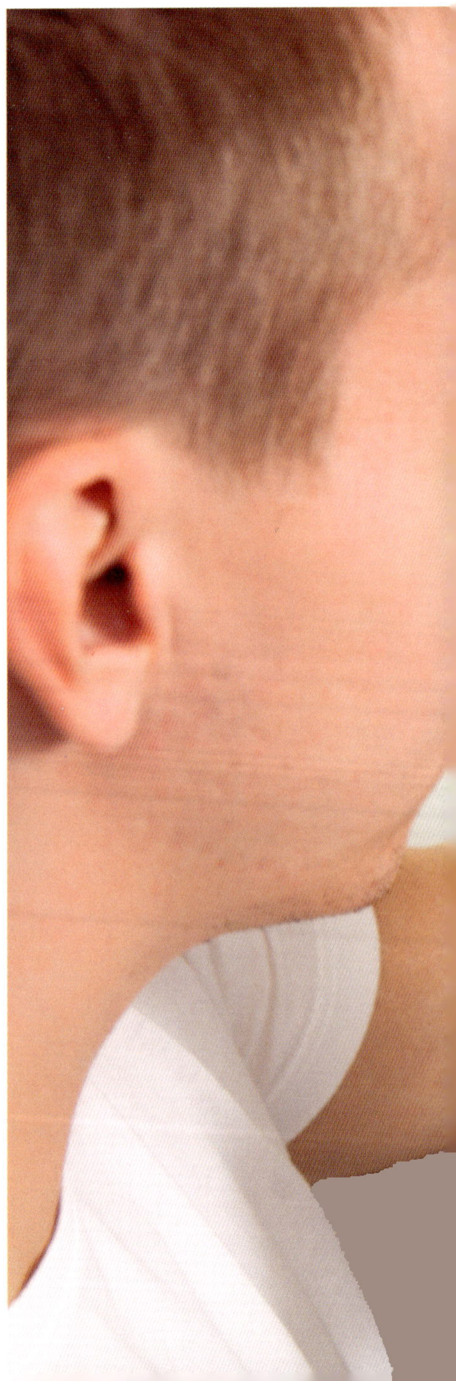

The art part of the job is evident in the finished product. Once restorations and appliances are made, lab technicians carefully shape and smooth them so they look and feel natural. They use a variety of equipment and hand tools: grinders, carvers, files, and polishers. Dental lab technicians combine scientific and mathematical precision with artistic flair.

TRENDS IN TECHNOLOGY

As in many practical science fields, technological advances are constantly being made in dentistry, particularly in the production of

A dental lab technician uses the cast of a patient's teeth and a milling machine to make crowns that fit perfectly and look natural.

cosmetic and restorative devices. New materials and new manufacturing methods are in use or in development, and technicians must learn how to work with the new products and technologies. In particular, modern lab technicians need some mastery of computer science. Digital technology permitted by computers is transforming the dental laboratory.

Dental restoration and correction always begins with an impression and a model of the patient's teeth. For decades, the impressions were made by having the patient bite down on a waxlike material. Today, dentists can maneuver a handheld camera, called an intra-oral scanner, inside the patient's mouth and generate a picture—a digital impression—of the patient's teeth. Because the digital impression is in 3D, it takes the place of a physical model.

How do dental techs construct a physical item to fit on an electronic image? They use computer-aided design (CAD) and computer-aided manufacturing (CAM). The intra-oral scanner has already captured all the information the technician needs to design the prosthesis, so the technician simply feeds the data into a CAD program. The program produces the design. CAM software then sends the information to a milling machine that carves or grinds the item from the dental material.

At present CAD/CAM technology is used only for simple restorations such as crowns and bridges. However, as the programs become more affordable and more dentists and technicians become comfortable using them, they are likely to become common and even preferred methods for making prostheses. However, these and the even more sophisticated technologies being developed are not likely to replace or reduce the need for dental lab technicians. When the milling machine produces a prosthesis, a technician must still smooth, polish, tint, and put other finishing touches on that prosthesis. Actually the advances are increasing the need for trained and skilled technicians. The technologies are simply programs, machinery,

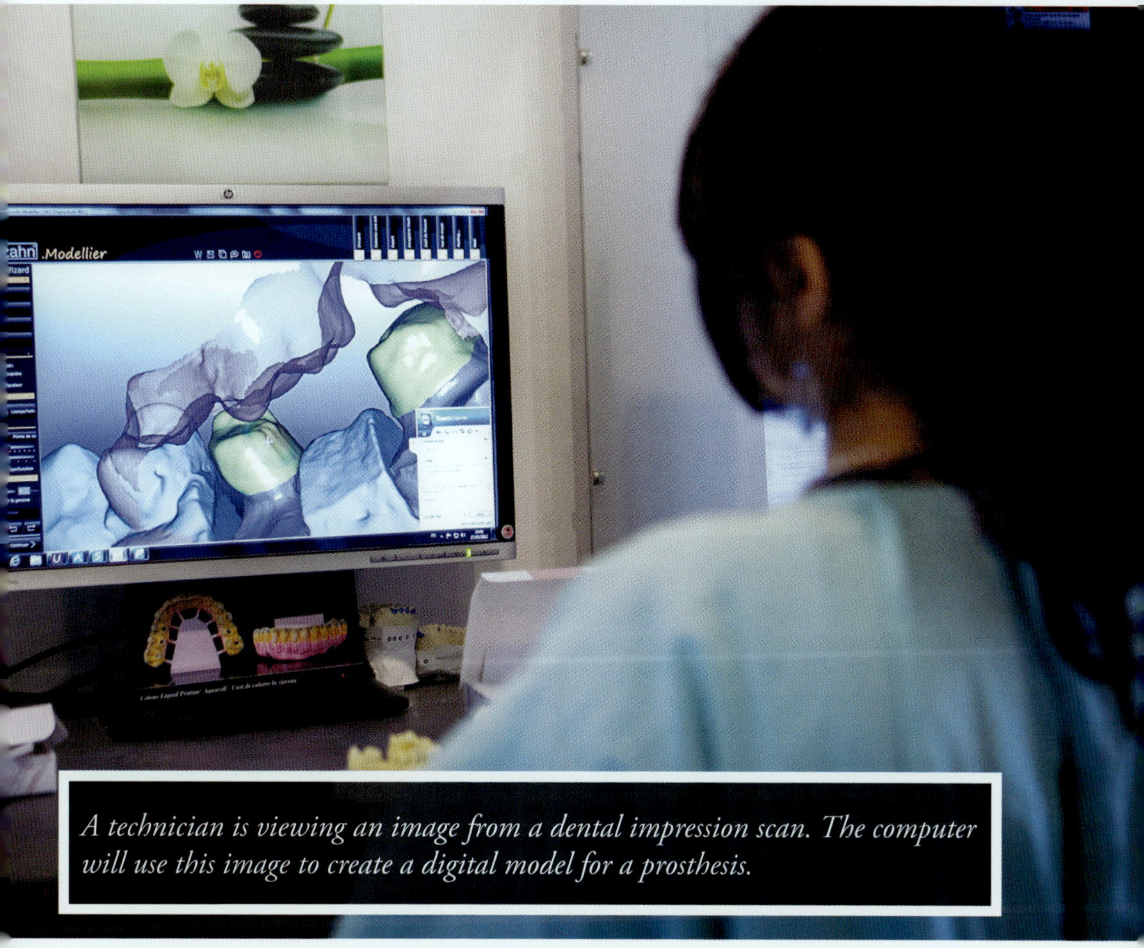

A technician is viewing an image from a dental impression scan. The computer will use this image to create a digital model for a prosthesis.

and processes that speed up the work, but technicians must still plan the production, operate the instruments, and perfect the final product.

Starting and Growing in a Career as a Dental Lab Technician

Despite the many skills required of a dental lab technician, this career path has one of the easiest starting points. All that is needed for an entry-level spot in many dental labs are a desire and an ability to do precision work—detailed work that must

NEW TEETH FROM A PRINTER?

In many dental offices today, getting a crown takes about two weeks and two visits. Typically, after the dentist prepares the tooth for a crown, a dental assistant makes an impression of the tooth and sends it off to a lab so a technician can fashion the crown. The patient gets a temporary crown at the first visit and a permanent crown when the lab has it ready.

However, some dentists can complete the entire process in a single one- or two-hour visit. They use cameras and computer-aided design (CAD) to scan and make a digital impression of the tooth and computer-aided manufacturing (CAM) to construct the crown. No putty in the mouth, no temporary, and no waiting.

The 3D printers are taking the process a step further. Usually crowns are milled. That is, the technician, dentist, or assistant takes a tooth-sized chunk of porcelain or other ceramic material and mills, or carves out, pieces to shape the crown. The 3D printers create the crown by layering micro threads of the ceramic material or of resin. Milling cuts away; printing builds up. Printing produces a crown that conforms more precisely to the tiny, intricate details of the patient's mouth and therefore fits and looks better.

The technology is still new and expensive, and the process of printing is considerably slower than milling. But the possibility of making longer-lasting and better-fitting dental products with less pain to patients is driving more research. Dentists look to the day when they can print not only crowns, but also bridges, dentures, orthodontic appliances, and more ... in their offices while their patients wait.

be exact—some artistic creativity, and a willingness to learn. Many laboratories hire high school graduates and train them on the job.

However, training is available and is relatively inexpensive. Community colleges, technical colleges, vocational schools, universities, and dental schools offer dental technology training programs accredited through the American Dental Association. Two-year programs award an associate's degree or a certificate, and four-year programs award a bachelor's degree. Graduates of these programs may not make significantly more money than on-the-job trainees initially, but they usually advance more quickly.

People who want to prove they have a professional level of knowledge and skills can become certified by the National Association of Dental Laboratories. To earn the certified dental technician certificate, they must pass three tests: a comprehensive exam, an exam in a specialty, and a hands-on practical exam. Certificates are available in six specialties: complete dentures, removable partial dentures, crown and bridge, ceramics, orthodontics, and implants. A person can earn one or more certifications. The National Association of Dental Laboratories provides study guides, practice exams, a list of study clubs, and other help for people considering or preparing for the tests. It also offers scholarships that cover the costs of the certification exams.

States do not license or register dental lab technicians, but they do license the laboratories. Some states will not permit a lab to operate unless it employs at least one certified dental technician. In those states, people who have obtained certification may stand a better chance of being hired.

Although the majority of dental lab technicians work in commercial laboratories, this career path, like other dental career paths, offers variety. A dental lab tech might work in a private dental office as a member of that office's oral health care team or in a hospital as part of a larger team. Companies that manufacture

This technician is creating a prosthesis in the large laboratory of the Boston University Dental Health Center.

dental devices and materials employ lab technicians.

Experienced technicians are needed to teach in dental laboratory technology education programs. Technicians who remain in the lab can advance beyond the tech job to supervisory and training positions. They may also own their own laboratories and employ additional technicians.

Even though people are taking better care of their teeth, the demand for dental lab techs is growing. A big part of the rising demand is in cosmetic dentistry. Veneers, crowns, and other cosmetic items have become more affordable, and more people are choosing to have optional items that improve their smiles. Adults who did not get braces as children are purchasing orthodontic appliances. The newer technologies enable dental lab technicians to create better products at faster speeds and lower cost, making this career path not only exciting, but also very secure.

chapter 5

Going Great Places

One reason dental careers are so exciting is the vast variety they offer. Although most dentists, hygienists, and dental assistants practice in small offices and most lab technicians work in mid-sized laboratories, opportunities are available in several other settings. The majority of dental practitioners choose to remain chairside, but some explore the myriad of other options available to them.

Practice Settings

About 90 percent of dentists, dental hygienists, and dental assistants work in private offices with one or two dentists. One of the dentists usually owns the practice and another may be an associate. Some dentists work as associates until they can afford to establish their own practices. In this traditional setting, some hygienists and assistants work full time and some work part time.

However, a trend is growing toward larger practices, many with more than twenty dentists and similar numbers of hygienists and assistants. Dentists with school debts to pay off may find working in a group practice preferable to trying to start their own businesses. Being employed by a dental corporation relieves them of the paperwork and the administrative tasks of operating a solo practice.

One advantage of a large dental practice is the ability to draw on the ideas and knowledge of a bigger team of dental professionals.

The typical setting for dental lab techs is also small—a laboratory with one to ten technicians. Often technicians own their labs. Some work in private dental offices and some in large dental corporations. There are also large commercial laboratories that employ more than a hundred technicians.

Outside the traditional office and lab, dental personnel work in hospitals, in military facilities, and for manufacturers and suppliers of dental products. The US Public Health Service employs dentists on Indian reservations, in federal prisons, and on US Coast Guard bases. People who are willing to practice in underserved areas can find jobs in public health settings:

community health centers, schools and preschools, juvenile halls, long-term care and assisted living facilities, group homes, and homeless shelters.

BEYOND CLINICAL PRACTICE

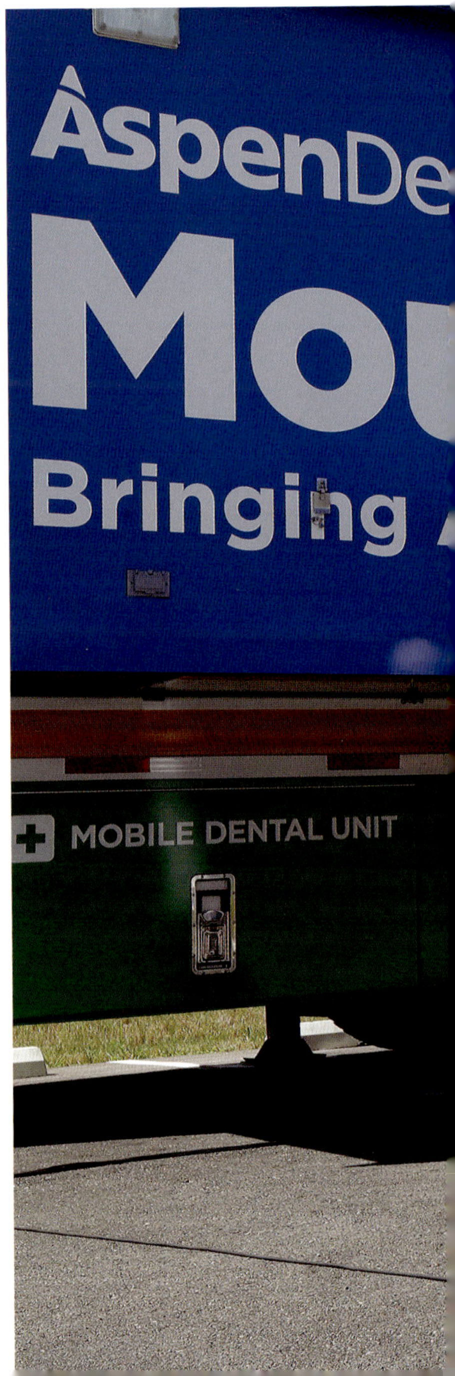

In addition to the variety in practice settings, dentists, hygienists, and lab techs can use their skills and knowledge in ways other than treating patients and creating prostheses and appliances. Opportunities are plentiful in teaching, research, and business and management. These can be part-time pursuits, added to clinical practice, or they can be full-time career pathways.

In the academic arena, dentists, hygienists, and lab techs can become instructors in dental education programs, training the next generation of practitioners. Or they can teach high school vocational classes that introduce students to career options. Dental hygienists are often asked to conduct seminars or classes on oral health in elementary schools, in health clinics, and at community events.

The American Dental Association is piloting a new career path called community dental health coordinator. It is for people who live in underserved communities who are or are willing to become hygienists and dental assistants. They are trained to provide education and

Race car driver Danica Patrick, a celebrity in this community in Indianapolis, Indiana, introduces the people who are bringing a one-day free dental clinic to people in need.

preventive services to the communities in which they live. The job combines education and some level of treatment.

Academic dentistry sometimes leads to careers in research. Universities and dental schools often have research departments that explore the latest in procedures, technology, materials, and products. Government agencies, private research companies, and companies that manufacture dental products all hire people to conduct research.

People with administrative skills as well as dentistry experience might enjoy managing a dental office, directing a dental hygiene program or a community clinic, or managing a company that makes dental products. They might like to work as consultants for a hospital, nursing home, or insurance company. Some enjoy selling dental products and equipment.

Forensic dentistry is another part-time endeavor or full-time career path. Forensic dentists examine dental remains and analyze bitemarks, often to identify victims of disasters and solve crimes. They also help historians understand and learn about people of the past.

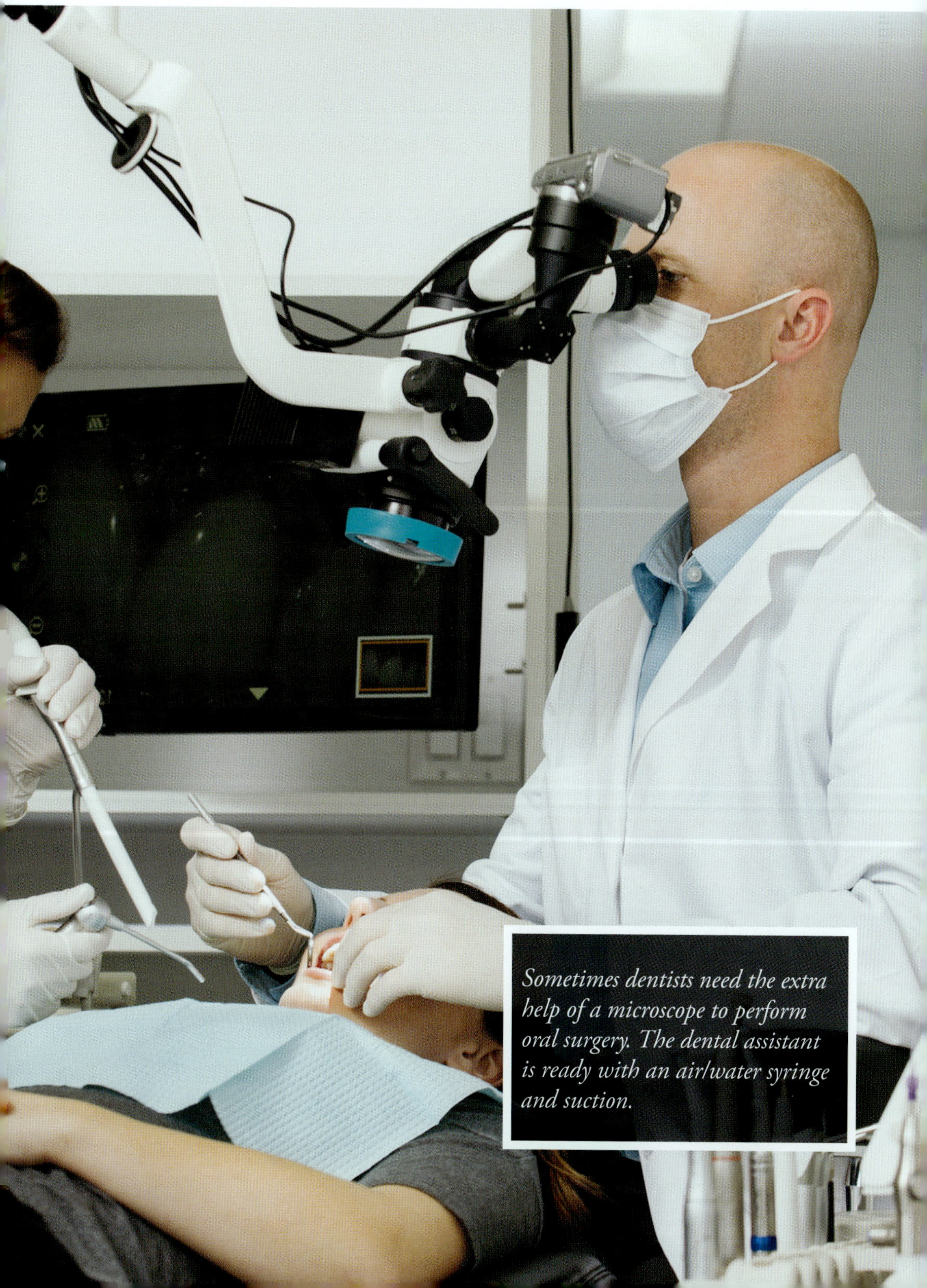

Sometimes dentists need the extra help of a microscope to perform oral surgery. The dental assistant is ready with an air/water syringe and suction.

A GOOD FIT FOR ME?

If any of these possibilities sounds appealing, you may be asking yourself if a dentistry career is for you. First you should consider whether you have the aptitude for the job; that is, whether your natural abilities and interests are suited to the kind of work you would be doing. Do you like working with your hands? Are you good at it? Dentists, hygienists, and dental assistants manipulate instruments in small spaces, and dental techs use hand tools to do delicate sculpting on small objects. They all have to have good finger dexterity as well as hand-eye coordination and good close-up vision.

Are you a problem solver? Dentists and hygienists evaluate patients' conditions and decide what to do about any problem they see. Technicians figure out how to translate a dentist's order or a computer image into porcelain or other material. Every patient and every order is a potential problem in need of a solution.

What about attention to detail? Do you notice little things? Part of the job of dental personnel is to spot abnormalities. Dentists and lab techs also have to note the details of teeth shape, color, and spacing.

And they have to concentrate on the patient or project in front of them, often for quite some time. Can you maintain your focus, or is it hard for you to stick with one thing for a long period? Some dental work is tedious; the job requires patience.

It also requires compassion. Some patients have situations that require special attention and some have fears. Dentists, hygienists, and assistants who work directly with patients should be sensitive and understanding. They must listen to patients and explain procedures and give instructions in a calm and confident manner. How are your people skills?

People skills are vital not only in regard to patients, but also with respect to others in the office. Dentists, hygienists,

At right is an example of a résumé for a dental lab technician. Someone with little experience applying for an entry-level position can list volunteer work on a résumé.

Ryan Smith

1365 Main Street • Omaha, NE 68120

(402) 437-8271 • rsmith4@gmail.com

OBJECTIVE

Begin work in a dental lab and develop skills as a dental lab technician

SUMMARY OF QUALIFICATIONS

- Artistic aptitude and skills
- Analytical thinker
- Detail oriented
- Skilled in using hand instruments
- Skilled in computer programming
- Good interpersonal skills
- Hard worker, eager to learn

RELATED EXPERIENCE

6/2015–present: Volunteer at Boys and Girls Club

- Help elementary school students understand and complete homework assignments
- Developed and conducted an art program teaching sculpting to fifteen students, including use of sculpting tools
- Help students design and build small cars for pinewood derby competition, including calculating weight placement for maximum speed
- Developed and conducted a program with twelve students designing and building model airplanes

2/2016 and 2/2017: Volunteer at UNMC Dental Day

- Before the event, helped assemble oral health care kits
- At the event, distributed kits to children

EDUCATION

- Benson High School, Omaha NE – graduated 2017

  Courses in math, biology, chemistry, woodshop, computer technology, art
- UNMC High School Alliance Health Sciences Enrichment Program, 2015–2016 and 2016–2017

  Courses: Exploration of Dental Medicine and Biomedical Research
- Summer Health Professions Education Program, summer 2016

SKILLS

- Sculpting, woodworking, use of small tools, computer programming assistants, and lab technicians are members of one team; they have to work together. Good communication is extremely important. Do you like working with others? Do others like working with you?

If you are not certain that you are suited for a dental career, taking an aptitude test will give you an idea of the type of job that is likely to be a good fit with your abilities and interests. Career planning centers of high schools, community colleges, and technical schools usually have these tests. Some dental programs require applicants to pass the Health Occupations Aptitude Exam before admittance. Some sample questions from this examination are available online; try answering those questions.

You can also get a feel for how you might like the job by seeing a dental office or laboratory in action. Contact your dentist, your school's career planning center, or the local chapter of a dental society to see who you might shadow or visit. If a dental school or dental training program is located in your area, you might be able to talk with students and faculty and learn something about training for a dental career.

Start Preparing Now

It is not too early to begin getting yourself ready for a career. Part of preparation is taking the right classes in high school. Dentistry is a science, so you should take science and math courses. Dentistry is a health science, so in addition to biology and chemistry, classes in anatomy, nutrition, and other health subjects will also be helpful. If you have an option of studying Latin, take it; it will help you learn and remember medical terms. Because dentistry is also an art, you might consider taking drawing, sculpting, drafting, and other art courses. Computer classes are also wise choices, especially if you are thinking about a dental technician career.

High school sculpting classes like this one develop finger dexterity, eye-hand coordination, artistic sense, attention to detail, and precision tooling, all helpful in dentistry.

It is also not too early to begin exploring training options. What dental education programs are located near you? What are their admissions requirements? How long do they take to complete and what do they cost? What financial help do they offer? You might want to start saving money toward your education now.

Another way to prepare, and to see how much you like dentistry, is to gain some experience. Without formal education in the field, the way to get experience is by volunteering. Volunteer in anything related to dentistry or health, even if the work is just stuffing envelopes or answering the phone. Just being in a

Volunteering helps you know if you will like the job field. It also lets you meet people who may be able to help you take the next step.

dental setting exposes you to the kinds of experiences you might expect in the job. Public health clinics, hospitals, assisted living facilities, and nursing homes frequently welcome help. Ask at your school's career planning center for volunteer opportunities.

If you can afford it, go on a short-term dental or medical mission. A number of organizations sponsor service projects in needy areas. The volunteer organization Project Abroad has a "High School Specials" division for youth ages sixteen to nineteen. The organization takes teams of young people to foreign countries to participate in short-term dental service projects.

Does your school encourage service learning projects? If so, why not develop a project for one of your classes? You might design and conduct an oral care education event or health fair at a preschool or elementary school. You could organize a drive to provide toothbrushes and tooth care products to a local shelter and enlist hygienists to volunteer for a day. Whatever you do—job shadow, volunteer, create a project—make sure to document it. In this way, you can begin building a portfolio that will help you when you are ready to apply for a dental education program or a job in the field.

Whenever you are ready, a job is likely to be waiting for you. The US Bureau of Labor Statistics foresees exceptionally good prospects for jobs in dentistry in the years ahead. In its predictions, which go to the year 2024, the bureau estimates the need for people in dental careers will continue to grow much faster than in many other industries. The national average for job growth is expected to be 7 percent, but jobs for dental lab technicians are projected to rise 10 percent; for dentists and dental assistants, 18 percent; and for dental hygienists, 19 percent. The job growth, together with high incomes, great flexibility, and high job satisfaction, makes a career in dentistry a great choice.

glossary

accredited Approved by a professional organization recognized as having the authority to establish high standards.

anatomy The science of the shape and structure of living beings or parts of living beings.

appliance A piece of equipment made for a specific purpose.

CAD/CAM The acronym for computer-aided design and computer-aided manufacturing, a method of designing and creating an object with the help of computer programs.

chairside Having to do with providing or assisting with dental treatment as the patient is seated in the dental treatment chair.

clinical Having to do with hands-on treatment of actual patients rather than theories about diseases or treatment.

denture A removable set of artificial teeth. A denture may be full, replacing all the top or bottom teeth, or partial, replacing some of the teeth.

enamel The hard outer layer of a tooth.

implant An artificial tooth on posts that is implanted, or inserted, into the jawbone as a replacement for a natural tooth.

milling The process of creating a crown or other item by carving or grinding it out of a piece of material.

orthodontics The dental specialty that treats improper alignment of teeth.

plaque A soft film that sticks to teeth, made up of food, bacteria, and other substances naturally found in the mouth.

prosthesis (plural **prostheses)** An artificial item or device use to replace or improve a damaged or missing part of the body.

radiograph An image produced by electromagnetic radiation, or X-rays.

resin A substance from trees or other plants used to make plastics, glues, and other products.

restorative dentistry The art and science of repairing or replacing damaged or missing teeth so they look and function as they should.

underserved The term used to describe an area or a group of people that does not have enough of a particular service (such as dental care) to meet its needs.

veneer A thin piece of material fixed to an object to protect it or improve its appearance.

for more information

American Dental Association (ADA)
211 East Chicago Avenue
Chicago, IL 60611-2678
(312) 440-2500
Website: http://www.ada.org
Facebook: @AmericanDentalAssociation
Twitter: @AmerDentalAssn
The ADA is the leading national association of dental professionals. The association provides accreditation for dental training programs and testing for dental certifications. Its website contains information on dental careers and programs as well as resources and information on oral health.

American Dental Education Association (ADEA)
655 K Street NW, Suite 800
Washington, DC 20001
(202) 289-7201
Website: http://www.adea.org
Facebook: @ADEAweb
Twitter: @adeaweb
ADEA is a national association of students, faculty, staff, and administrators of dental schools and other dental education programs in the United States and Canada. It publishes a guide to dental schools, a listing of scholarships and other financial awards, and other information about initial and ongoing dental education.

American Dental Hygienists' Association (ADHA)
444 North Michigan Avenue, Suite 3400
Chicago, IL 60611

(312) 440-8900
Website: https://www.adha.org
Facebook: @youradha
Twitter: @YourADHA
The ADHA is a professional organization of registered dental hygienists that provides information and resources supporting the practice of dental hygiene.

American Student Dental Association (ASDA)
211 East Chicago Avenue, Suite 700
Chicago, IL 60611-2678
(312) 440-2795 and (800) 621-8099, ext. 2795
Website: http://www.asdanet.org
Facebook: @asda.net
The ASDA is a national, student-led organization of dental students that provides information, education, services, and representation to dental students and people interested in becoming students.

Canadian Dental Association (CDA)
1815 Alta Vista Drive
Ottawa, ON K1G 3Y6
Canada
(613) 523-1770
Website: https://www.cda-adc.ca/en
Facebook: @CanadianDentalAssociation
Twitter: @CdnDentalAssoc
A federation of the dental associations of Canada's provinces, the CDA provides information on oral health to the general public and resources on education and practice for dentists and dental students.

Canadian Dental Hygienist Association (CDHA)
1122 Wellington Street W
Ottawa, ON K1Y 2Y7
Canada
(800) 267-5235 and (613) 224-5515
Website: http://www.cdha.ca
Facebook: @theCDHA
Twitter: @theCDHA
The CDHA is a professional organization of dental hygienists that provides information on the practice of oral health care as well as careers, education, and news related to oral health.

National Association of Dental Laboratories (NADL)
325 John Knox Road
Tallahassee, FL 32303
(800) 950-1150
Website: https://nadl.org
The NADL serves the needs of the dental laboratory industry. It provides resources, information, continuing education, networking opportunities, and other programs and services to people interested or engaged in the profession.

Websites

Because of the changing nature of internet links, Rosen Publishing has developed an online list of websites related to the subject of this book. This site is updated regularly. Please use this link to access the list:

http://www.rosenlinks.com/ECAR/Dentist

for further reading

Brooks, Janine. *How to Develop Your Career in Dentistry.* Chichester, UK: John Wiley & Sons, 2015.

Byers, Ann. *A Career As a Dental Hygienist* (Essential Careers). New York, NY: Rosen Publishing, 2013.

Hoskins, Jamie. *Becoming a Dentist in the U.S.: A Guide to Becoming a Dentist.* CreateSpace Publishing, 2016.

Institute for Career Research. *Your Career As a Dental Hygienist.* CreateSpace Publishing, 2016.

Johnson, Ann. *Dental Assistant Career: The Insider's Guide to Finding a Job at an Amazing Firm, Acing the Interview and Getting Promoted.* CreateSpace Publishing, 2016.

Johnson, Ann. *Dental Laboratory Technician Career: The Insider's Guide to Finding a Job at an Amazing Firm, Acing the Interview and Getting Promoted.* CreateSpace Publishing, 2016.

Morrison, Janie. *How to Get a Job and Succeed as a Dentist.* Bull City Publishing, 2015.

Rule, James T., and Muriel J. Bebeau. *Dentists Who Care: Inspiring Stories of Professional Commitment*. Hanover Park, IL: Quintessence, 2005.

Saval, Malina. *Dental Hygienist: Stories from People Who've Done It.* 101 Publishing, 2012.

US Air Force. *Dental Assistant Specialty: Air Force Career Education and Training Plan.* BiblioGov, 2012.

US Air Force. *Dental Laboratory Specialty: Air Force Career Education and Training Plan.* BiblioGov, 2012.

US Department of Labor. *Young Person's Occupational Outlook Handbook*. 7th ed. Indianapolis, IN: JIST Works, Inc., 2010.

bibliography

American Dental Association. "Expanded Functions for Dental Assistants." March 28, 2011. http://www.aapd.org/assets/1/7/StateLawsonDAs.pdf.

American Dental Association. *Fast-Track Training: The Basics for Dental Staff.* Chicago, IL: American Dental Association, 2007.

American Dental Hygienists' Association. *Competencies for the Advanced Dental Hygiene Practitioner (ADHP).* Chicago, IL: American Dental Hygienists' Association, 2008. https://www.adha.org/resources-docs/72612_ADHP_Competencies.pdf.

Decker, Bill. "3D Printing Dentistry Gets Faster and Faster." *Dental Market*, 2015. http://3dprintingdentalmarket.com/3d-printing-dental-news/.

FDI World Dental Federation. "FDI's Definition of Oral Health." Retrieved February 13, 2017. http://www.fdiworldental.org/oral-health/vision-2020/fdis-definition-of-oral-health.aspx.

Interview with Dr. Gary Eritzian, DDS. Fresno, California, February 5, 2017.

Mayo Clinic. "Dental Exam." February 14, 2015. http://www.mayoclinic.org/tests-procedures/dental-exam/basics/what-you-can-expect/prc-20013677.

Otto, Mary. "For Want of a Dentist." *Washington Post*, February 28, 2007. http://www.washingtonpost.com/wp-dyn/content/article/2007/02/27/AR2007022702116.html.

Phillip, Abby. "A Trip to the Dentist Helped Uncover an 11-year-old's Grapefruit-sized Tumor and Saved Her

Life." *Washington Post*, February 13, 2015. https://www.washingtonpost.com/news/to-your-health/wp/2015/02/13/a-trip-to-the-dentist-helped-uncover-a-grapefruit-sized-tumor-and-saved-this-11-year-old-girls-life/?utm_term=.cf383c9ece1f.

Reynolds, Anije Seewer. "The Making of a Dentist: A Story of Love and Teeth." WorkLifeGroup. Retrieved January 12, 2017. http://career.worklifegroup.com/career-stories/making-dentist-story-love-and-teeth-anije-seewer-reynolds-86.html.

US Bureau of Labor Statistics. "Dental Assistants." *Occupational Outlook Handbook, 2016–2017 Edition*. Retrieved January 12, 2017. https://www.bls.gov/ooh/healthcare/dental-assistants.htm.

US Bureau of Labor Statistics. "Dental Hygienists." *Occupational Outlook Handbook, 2016–2017 Edition*. Retrieved January 12, 2017. https://www.bls.gov/ooh/healthcare/dental-hygienists.htm.

US Bureau of Labor Statistics. "Dental and Ophthalmic Laboratory Technicians and Medical Appliance Technicians." *Occupational Outlook Handbook, 2016–2017 Edition*. Retrieved January 12, 2017. https://www.bls.gov/ooh/production/dental-and-ophthalmic-laboratory-technicians-and-medical-appliance-technicians.htm.

US Bureau of Labor Statistics. "Dentists." *Occupational Outlook Handbook, 2016–2017 Edition*. Retrieved January 12, 2017. https://www.bls.gov/ooh/healthcare/dentists.htm.

"*U.S. News and World Report* Announces the 1017 Best Jobs." *U.S. News and World Report*, January 11, 2017. http://www.usnews.com/info/blogs/press-room/articles/2017-01-11/us-news-announces-the-2017-best-jobs.

Valochovic, Richard. *Current Demographics and Future Trends of the Dental Workforce.* National Academies, 2009. http://www.nationalacademies.org/hmd/~/media/Files/Activity%20Files/Workforce/oralhealthworkforce/2009-Feb-09/1%20-%20Valachovic.ashx.

index

ABOUT THE AUTHOR

As a youth worker in low-income and minority communities, Ann Byers has long been concerned with youth employment. She pioneered an inner-city job club, teaching employability skills, and organized job fairs and conferences. Her book on application, résumé, and interview skills has helped first-time job seekers enter the workforce. She has explored several careers for young people to consider, writing, among other books, *Jobs as Green Builders and Planners*, *A Career as a Dental Hygienist*, *Jump-Starting a Career in Dietetics and Nutrition*, and *A Career as a Construction Manager*.

PHOTO CREDITS

Cover (figure) LattaPictures/E+/Getty Images; cover (background) Photographee.eu/Shutterstock.com; p. 4 Solis Images/Shutterstock.com; pp. 8–9 Monkey Business Images/Shutterstock.com; pp. 12–13 Jasminko Ibrakovic/Shutterstock.com; pp. 14–15 Sheila Fitzgerald/Shutterstock.com; pp. 16–17 Spencer Platt/Getty Images; pp. 18–19 Ancika/iStock/Thinkstock; pp. 22–23 RichLegg/E+/Getty Images; pp. 24–25 Andrey Popov/Shutterstock.com; pp. 28–29 © iStockphoto.com/Choja; p. 31 Bloomberg/Getty Images; pp. 34–35 wavebreakmedia/Shutterstock.com; p. 37 Lighthaunter/iStock/Thinkstock; p. 40 bikeriderlondon/Shutterstock.com; pp. 42–43 Lucky Business/Shutterstock.com; pp. 46–47 Ocskay Bence/Shutterstock.com; pp. 48–49 danielzgombic/E+/Getty Images; p. 51 BSIP/Universal Images Group/Getty Images; pp. 54–55 Matilde Gattoni/ArabianEye/Getty Images; p. 57 Bojan89/iStock/Thinkstock; pp. 58–59 © AP Images; pp. 60-61 Erik Isakson/Getty Images; p. 65 Blend Images-Hill Street Studios/Brand X Pictures/Getty Images; p. 66 Mangostock/Shutterstock.com.

Design: Matt Cauli; Layout: Tahara Anderson; Senior Editor: Kathy Kuhtz Campbell; Photo Research: Sherri Jackson